Finding Somewhere

Also by

Joseph Monninger

Wish

Hippie Chick

Baby

Finding Somewhere

Joseph Monninger

DELACORTE PRESS

Text copyright © 2011 by Joseph Monninger
Jacket art copyright © 2011 by Veer

All rights reserved. Published in the United States by Delacorte Press, an imprint of Random House Children's Books, a division of Random House, Inc., New York.

Delacorte Press is a registered trademark and the colophon is a trademark of Random House, Inc.

Visit us on the Web! www.randomhouse.com/teens

Educators and librarians, for a variety of teaching tools, visit us at www.randomhouse.com/teachers

Library of Congress Cataloging-in-Publication Data
Monninger, Joseph.
Finding somewhere / Joseph Monninger. — 1st ed.
p. cm.
Summary : Sixteen-year-old Hattie and eighteen-year-old Delores set off on a road trip that takes unexpected turns as they discover the healing power of friendship and confront what each of them is fleeing from.
ISNB 978-0-385-73942-9 (hc : alk. paper) — ISBN 978-0-375-86214-4 (ebook) — ISBN 978-0-385-90789-7 (glb : alk. paper)
[1. Coming of age—Fiction. 2. Friendship—Fiction. 3. Automobile travel—Fiction.] I. Title.
PZ7.M7537Fi 2011
[Fic]—dc22
2010053551

The text of this book is set in 12-point Tibere.

Book design by Jinna Shin

Printed in the United States of America

10 9 8 7 6 5 4 3 2 1

First Edition

To all girls who love horses

Finding Somewhere

And Allah took a handful of southerly wind, blew His breath over it, and created the horse. . . . Thou shall fly without wings, and conquer without sword. O horse!

—BEDOUIN LEGEND

Chapter 1

I SLIPPED THROUGH THE GATE WITHOUT ANY PROBLEM AND heard the horses shift and move the way they do when something unfamiliar comes into their space. I knew the stable, of course, and I felt bad for sneaking in, but the Fergusons hadn't left me much choice in the matter. Luckily, a full moon gave me enough light. I walked quickly across the first paddock, where we usually saddled them, and Bucker looked over his stall and whinnied. I said, "Shhhhh," but he whinnied again, greedy bugger that he is, and I slipped close and gave him an apple. He chomped it the way he always does, the big blockheaded fool, but I kissed him on his star forehead and told him to be quiet.

"I'm here for Speed," I said. "Not you."

He slobbered over the apple. It was late September in New Hampshire, the leaves falling into tall grass. You could bite the air. You couldn't blame a horse for feeling it. The air made us all crazy.

I DIDN'T TURN ON ANY LIGHTS. I WALKED DOWN THE boardwalk outside the stable doors and I gave a quick pat to the horses I passed. Pumpkin, Sally, Clumpy, Bees, Wally, and Sammy. Speed dozed in the second-to-last stall, next to Sammy, and he didn't even wake when I stood right in front of him.

"What a lazy bucket you are," I said when I reached for him.

I put my arms around him and he drooped his head over my shoulder and nuzzled his chin against my back. Other horses sometimes let you hug them, but Speed was the only horse I'd ever known who hugged back. He clamped me to him, his chin pulling me closer, and I held him for a little while and whispered what we were going to do. I told him I loved him, too, and he kept pressure on my back as though he were listening. As though he understood. Then I blew into his ear a little, to get it flicking, and he made a soft, gentle sound deep in his belly.

"Who's my boy?" I whispered to him. "Who's my favorite horse in the whole world? Who's my good, good boy?"

I kissed him on his cheek and on his forehead. Then I grabbed his halter and clipped a lead to it, and swung the stall door open. He plodded out, a big horse still, nearly sixteen hands at the withers, but old, and he walked quietly. He had manners. Everyone who had ever ridden him—and a million people had ridden him—knew that. He didn't kick or bite or fight the bit. His gentleness surprised you a little, because of his size, and if you didn't know better you expected him to go back on it, but he never did. True blue, really. I got him out and rubbed his ears and forehead a little, then put my ear against his cheek.

"You want to go for a ride?" I asked Speed. "You want to get out of here?"

He didn't, of course. No horse wants to leave a warm stall on a fall night to go walking in the dark.

He didn't know it was his last night alive. A horse doesn't know that kind of thing, even though it knows a whole lot more.

I TUCKED $240 ON THE HOOK OF THE SADDLE PEG IN Speed's stable. That was what I figured the saddle was worth. I had written a note, too, but now I debated about leaving it. I had spent a long time composing it, trying to strike the right tone. The Fergusons are good people, and good horse people, too, so I didn't want to hurt their feelings. I had worked for them two years, almost steadily, doing everything around the stables a person could do. I'd grown up in their barn, really, and I knew they weren't trying to be cold or uncaring about Speed. They figured he was broke for good and they had Carter, their grounds man, dig a pit grave with his backhoe out in the bones pasture. They had considered letting Speed live through the winter, but if a horse dies in the New Hampshire winter, you can't dig a grave for him—sometimes not even with a backhoe. It's a mess. They had come to a decision, and I didn't exactly blame them for it, but I believe a horse, or any animal, should have a chance to live as long as it has dignity. If it can't eat, or has horrible tumors—and I've worked with horses with both problems—then a merciful end is justified. But Speed's problem wasn't anything like that. He had gone dead in his heart, I felt, and didn't have much joy left, because for most of his life he had been treated like a machine. He worked in fairs, on pony ride circuits, at a horseback riding academy when he was younger. A horse-slave, Mr. Ferguson said about horses like Speed. The Fergusons had taken his body in, but not his heart.

I left the note on the hook with the money. I didn't want anyone to be confused about my motives. I didn't want the Fergusons to think I had betrayed them. It wasn't like I had a long, carefully planned plot in my head. I didn't want them to have that idea. I had decided to take Speed because I had to.

> *Dear Mr. & Mrs. Ferguson,*
>
> *I am taking Speed on a little vacation. Don't worry, I've got it figured out. I'll take good care of him. I left $240 for the saddle, which I hope is fair, and if it isn't, I'll make it up to you in work. I hope you understand. Sorry to do this, but I couldn't stand by and let Speed go down tomorrow. Sorry. No offense. I'll be back in a month or two, and if you still want me to work for you, I'd like that. If not, I understand.*
>
> *Hattie Wyatt*

MY NOTE DIDN'T INCLUDE A WHOLE CATALOG OF THINGS. I didn't say, for instance, that I hoped to let Speed be a horse for once. That I took Speed so he could have a chance to live on a prairie for a season, one fall, and that I'd love him and protect him. I didn't say that Delores was coming, too, because they knew Delores, understood that she was as horse crazy as I was, but wasn't necessarily someone you hired. I didn't say that we had plans to take her truck, that Delores had been kicked out of her house, or had been "invited to leave," as she put it, and that she might keep going toward California. Over time I've learned you don't tell people more than they need to know. I didn't tell them we had over a thousand dollars saved and we had toyed with the idea of a cross-country trip for quite a while, but that Speed's death sentence gave us a final push. I kept that to myself.

I slid the saddle over Speed and pulled the gut straps tight. Speed didn't shudder or protest or play any tricks like holding his belly full, then letting it slink when you climbed on him. He was too sound for that, and I felt, I don't know, that I might have even welcomed a trick or two from him just by way of protest. He had his entire life to protest, and never did, and as soon as I climbed on his back I bent forward and told him I loved him. I whispered that he was my boy, my good horse. As gently as I could, I prodded him forward. He clopped ahead and then paused, not sure where to go. I kicked him a little more and said, "Come on, Speed," and he did as I asked because that's what he does.

We rode down the Fergusons' long driveway. It was beautiful. The Fergusons made their money down in Boston and retired up here to New Hampshire, and they had the kind of dough that let them plant trees down a long driveway and hire people like Carter, and take in horses from the Humane Society. They did good things with their wealth, no dispute, but sometimes they didn't notice that their hobbies made other people's hands stay awfully busy. Maybe that isn't fair, I don't know, but Mr. Ferguson made money by trading on the stock exchange, and that was a different kind of work than digging fence postholes or cleaning stables, and he didn't see that. He figured he was being okay with people—kind of like he rescued people from the Humane Society right along with the horses and llamas they cared for—but the help always came tied to a kind of work that reflected back the right way on the Fergusons. Sometimes thinking about them tied me up.

Speed clopped ahead anyway. I wanted him to give some sign of liberation, but I knew if I dropped the reins he would turn slowly around and go back to his stable. Horses are like people that way.

NEW HAMPSHIRE SUGAR MAPLES. THAT'S THE KIND OF trees the Fergusons had had planted along the road, and they were adolescent trees, but pretty, too, and going over toward fall. A wild night, my uncle Ed used to call nights like this one, when the moon is full and woodsmoke lips out of the chimneys. I rubbed Speed's neck and told him to take a good, deep breath, but he just kept going slowly. He had spent about seven years at a kids' pony ride place over in Dunbarton, and still, whenever he came to a left-hand track, he took it, thinking it was the circle he had had to plod with some birthday kid on his back and a mom running beside with a camera. That was the kind of thing that got to me about Speed.

We didn't come to any left-hand turns, though. I pulled him right at the end of the driveway and kicked him a little to get him going. He took two steps a little faster, then settled back into his walk. The moon stayed up ahead of us.

"HELLO, SPEEDY," DELORES SAID.

She came forward and rubbed his nose and forehead. She wore a headlamp, so the beam went wherever she looked.

When she glanced up at me, all I could see was light. When I climbed off Speed, though, I saw her in the good moonlight. She looked excited. She looked pretty, too, the way her reddish hair picked up the light and her skin seemed bright and white and tied to the moon somehow. She had taken off some weight recently, and she moved with quick, easy motions that made me think of a broom touching the ground. She wore about a dozen friendship bracelets that people had given her, and whenever she reached up to touch Speed, her wrists flashed braided strings. She always liked little things like that, and she reminded me of a Christmas tree sometimes, only a tree in a household that didn't have much, a tree that had to be decorated with popcorn strings and clothespin animals rather than fancy crystal balls and soft white lights. There was always a little something "make-do" about Delores, something thrift-store and sub-retail, and that wouldn't have been bad except you could tell it sometimes got to her and made her self-conscious and lonely in her head.

"Any trouble?" she asked.

"Nope," I said. "Not a thing."

"Let's get him in," she said. "We'll be out of the state by dawn."

"Okay," I said, and I kissed his nose.

We unsaddled Speed in no time, then rubbed him down

quickly. Delores had taken a horse trailer from Gray's Farm, her cousin's place. She had put a bale of hay up on the eating rack so Speed could eat what he liked as he rode. We lined Speed up and led him inside. He went right up the ramp without a thought. He filled up the trailer, though, and it took us a second to close him off in the rear.

"He's done that a couple million times," I said.

"Sure has," Delores said.

She latched the back with a padlock, then scooted around to the driver's side. I climbed in and checked behind me. I couldn't see Speed.

When Delores slid in, she was wired the way she gets sometimes. She had a manic energy that made people like the Fergusons nervous around her. They found her too much, too excitable. A lot of people did. But I didn't. She was like a wind that came over the White Mountains, all nutty and strong, but she could be calm, too. Delores wasn't all one thing.

"Okay," she said. "No surrender."

I nodded. She started the engine and pointed us west.

"WE DID IT!" DELORES SAID WHEN WE HAD GONE ABOUT A mile. "We freaking did it! I can't believe, after all the talk, we finally did it."

She tapped the steering wheel, playing along with Coldplay, the band she idolized. I could tell she felt good. She wore jeans and an old ratty sweater she liked and had her hair up in a baseball hat. She wore a blue down vest over the sweater, and her pair of Doc Martens. She was revved.

"We're going west," I said. "And Speed, too."

"Old Speedy," she said. "Your Speedy."

"What do you think they'll say when they find the note?"

"The Fergies? Oh, they'll be glad to have the horse off their hands."

"They're not like that," I said.

"You're right," Delores said. "They're worse."

"Come on."

"What are they going to say, Hattie? You didn't steal anything of value. They were going to put Speed down tomorrow. So now they won't have to. They'll tsk and call your mom, and that will be that. Then your mom will call my mom and they'll piece it together. By that time we'll be west of Chicago or something."

"I'd hate to make them feel bad. They've been good to me."

"Oh, they'll like feeling indignant and everything else. It'll give them something to do. They always figure we're a bunch of crazy people living up here in trailers. You know. Trashy. This will make them feel superior."

"You're cynical," I said. "They like you, too, you know."

"They're not sure what to make of me, Hattie. They figure I'll be pregnant and on food stamps in about a year. They still have a little hope for you."

"You're full of it."

"Road trip!" she yelled, and I had to smile. "The heck with everything else."

It was a magical night. The moon shone right on the road, and we followed it, almost as though it were tempting us to catch it. We took back roads, just in case, and kept her Ford F-150 at an easy pace. On both sides of us the trees had begun to turn. My mom always listened to the foliage report, the track the autumn colors made from the north down. Peak for our region still remained a couple weeks away, but driving, I realized it didn't matter. I wouldn't be here.

We drove for a long time. Eventually we stopped talking, and the road hypnotized us. The whole world shrank down to a white line on a black piece of ribbon going through trees. My mind washed around to different things—the Fergusons, Mom, our house, Marbles my cat, the GED course where Delores and I had met and become friends—but it never settled on one thing. We had a leaving feeling, that's what it was.

"What time is it?" Delores asked eventually. "You hungry?"

"It's around four."

"There's a place I know that's not too far. Right near the Vermont border. Why don't we stop for breakfast?"

"I want to check Speed, too."

She nodded.

"You know," she said, "if I had a lot of money, I'd buy about a thousand acres out in Wyoming and I'd leave it empty. Just as empty as it could be. And I'd put out the word that anyone who had an old horse could just swing by and drop that horse off. Nature would take care of the rest. I wouldn't allow anything but horses."

"There are places like that," I said. "I found some online."

"I mean really free horse country. Prairie land. What do you think Speed will do when he sees a prairie?"

"He's old," I said.

"You wait," she said. "There's some life left in him. No more going in circles. Speedy boy is going to be free as a bird."

Then for a little while Delores did a dance that she does when she's feeling goofy. It's a kind of wiggle thing where she pretends the gear shift is her partner, and she did some finger waves and some voodoo passes, and she reached over and made me do it, too. She goes high and she goes low, Delores.

She was in an up phase, I knew, but that could turn around. I'd seen her change in five minutes flat, go from bubbly to sad in the time it takes to walk to the kitchen in most houses. Right now, with the sun just starting to scrape back the night, she danced like a crazy woman. "Full moon, full moon, full moon," she chanted. And for a while she drove with her knees, her hands throwing themselves at the world around her. Now and then I spotted the slits in her wrists—the scars, deep scars going up and down vertically the way the serious ones try it—and wished that she would hold on and go a little slower, breathe a little deeper, find a center place and try to be there.

Chapter 2

DELORES ORDERED PANCAKES WITH SAUSAGE. I ORDERED A cheese omelet with home fries and cinnamon toast. We split a pot of tea.

"That be all for now?" the waitress asked after she delivered the meals. "You got everything you need?"

She was a big woman with breasts the size of dachshunds. You had to make a deliberate effort to raise your eyes above the cliff they made. Her name tag said *Sue*.

"We're set," I said. "Thank you."

"Don't see many girls out this time of morning," Sue said. "Nice to have a break from all the truckers."

"We're delivering a horse," I said, which was a phrase we had scripted to have on hand for anyone asking.

"Well, good for you. Call me over if you need anything."

She took off. Delores dripped honey over her pancakes. She hated maple syrup, I knew.

"Speed looked good," she said as she speared some pancake. "He's used to riding in a trailer."

"How many days, you think?" I asked, even though we had discussed it a thousand times since Speed had received his death sentence.

"Four days, maybe. Depends how we go. If we take turns driving, no problem."

"You think they'll call the police?"

Delores stabbed pancake and then sausage.

"Who knows? I'll be honest, I'm more worried about my cousin whistling me down for the trailer than I am about Speed. The Fergies aren't the sort to want the police to know their private business."

"I've got to call Mom this morning. She'll have a hissy."

"But in the end, what can she do?"

"I'm not eighteen," I said.

"I am," Delores said.

"Which makes you arrestable."

"Is 'arrestable' a word? Pass me the butter, would you?"

I did. I ate some of my omelet. It was pretty good, though the cook had tried to fancy it up by sprinkling paprika on it. The home fries were better. We ate and watched the truckers slide into booths here and there around the diner. Most of them were fat. Sue scuttled around serving everyone. She brought coffee before anyone asked for it. She carried the white cups in bunches.

"How far do you think we can get today?" I asked after we had eaten half our meal.

"Ohio, maybe."

"You ever been out West?" I asked.

Delores shook her head.

"Nope," she said.

"You think it looks like it does in the movies?"

"Nothing looks like anything does in the movies."

"Except Johnny Depp."

"If Johnny Depp in real life looked like Johnny Depp in the movies, people would faint around him."

"Girls," I said.

"Heck, gay guys would, too."

"My mom used to always say, 'Life isn't a movie.' That

was supposed to be a cure for something. Like you shouldn't believe in appearances."

"You really think your mom is going to throw a hissy?" Delores asked.

"Of course. You know how she is."

"My mom will say she expected something like this. She'll say it's harebrained. What is harebrained, anyway?"

"No idea."

"No one who loves horses will think it's harebrained."

A pair of youngish truckers slid into the booth behind Delores. They had big belt buckles and wide sideburns. They smelled of cigarettes and diesel. Delores started speaking French to me. She couldn't really speak it, but it was something we did. Sometimes on ski lifts or in a mall we spoke pretend French, throwing in a word and mumbling things together so that it almost sounded like something. That's what she did now. I answered back, running my voice up and down French scales, trying to sound Parisian. After a while the guy closest to us turned in his seat and asked if we were from Montreal.

"No," Delores said.

She said it *non,* like a Frenchy.

"Where, then?" the guy said.

"Paree," Delores said.

"Paris?" the guy asked.

"*Oui.*"

That made us laugh, and the guy turned back to his table and left us alone. Then Delores started making kissing poses by sticking out her lips and closing her eyes. She meant it as a commentary on the guys, mocking them, but finally Sue came with the check.

"You girls drive careful," Sue said, tearing off the check.

"We will," I said.

"What kind of horse, anyway?"

"A chestnut named Speed."

"Well, here," she said, handing us a plastic bag of carrots. "The cook said he had extra."

"Thank you," I said. "That's really nice."

"I like horses," she said.

We left a good tip, then slid out of the booth. The trucker guy who had spoken to us said, *"Au revoir."*

"À bientôt," Delores said to him.

"Inky dinky *parlez-vous,*" the second driver said.

We linked arms and ran outside. We laughed all the way out to the truck. Delores, the happy Delores. Delores the pretend French-speaking Delores. We kept swinging around and around, like two planets slinging away from the sun. The light had just cleared the White Mountains behind us.

"MOM?" I SAID.

"Where in the world are you?" she asked.

We were parked in a rest stop not far from Albany. We had already crossed Vermont. Delores had stopped for a bathroom break, and when I checked her cell phone, it had three bars. I called home.

"I'm in New York State," I said.

"With Delores, of course."

"Yes," I said.

"You girls are going to be the death of me."

I didn't say anything.

"The Fergusons called here first thing this morning," Mom said, her voice becoming businesslike. "They're quite upset with you."

"Sorry."

"Sorry doesn't really cut it, does it?"

"They were going to kill Speed."

"They don't think the horse is in any condition for a road trip. They think you'll actually be cruel to the horse by taking it somewhere."

"I'd never be cruel to a horse. You know that."

"You wouldn't mean to be, Hattie. But sometimes your judgment might fall a little short."

We didn't say anything for a second. Delores returned. She had a water bottle. She sat on the hood of the truck and drank.

"We'll take care of the horse," I said.

"You're too young to be riding around the country on your own."

"I'm with Delores."

"Is that supposed to reassure me? Delores has a history of being fragile, Hattie. We both know that."

"It's only a couple weeks."

I heard her breathe out smoke. It was easy to picture her on the back porch, a cigarette in one hand, a cup of coffee in the other, the phone tucked between her chin and shoulder. It was a Wednesday, so she had the midmorning shift at the parts store. She had to be at work at ten.

"Just when I thought things were a little on track with you," she said. "You just earned your GED. I thought we were heading somewhere."

"I am heading somewhere."

"Not in a straight line, I'll tell you that."

"Mom, it's only going to be a couple weeks. Then we'll be back."

"Delores, too? Because her mom is going to call, and I better know what to say."

"Her mom wants her out of there. Her mom has a new boyfriend."

"So she's not coming back? So you won't just be a couple weeks necessarily."

"She's not sure."

"Well, that's just great. And how will you get back?"

"I'll take a bus."

"And where are you actually going? Do you know?"

"I have a couple places in mind."

"The Fergusons think the trailer ride will be too much for Speed."

"He's doing fine. We just checked him."

"This is just crazy, Hattie."

"Not that crazy, Mom. I'm not trying to be defiant. I just knew if I asked people for permission they wouldn't give it."

"By 'people,' you mean me?"

"You or the Fergusons."

"It's their horse, by the way."

"It would be dead by now," I said. "So any way you count it, he's doing better with us."

"You wear me out, Hattie."

"I don't mean to."

She didn't say anything. I looked at Delores. She had the water bottle to her lips. People pulled in and pulled out. I heard Speed move in the trailer. We needed to get him out of there soon and give him a break.

"Do you have some sort of plan for your life other than stealing horses?" Mom asked.

"I'm sixteen, Mom. I don't have a life plan."

"I just wish you'd think more before you do things. This is the kind of impulsive behavior we've talked about before. Delores feeds right into that."

"I know I'm sometimes impulsive, Mom. But not about this. Delores and I figured everything out."

"I want you to turn around and come back, Hattie," Mom said. "What in the world do you suppose people will think of a mother who lets her sixteen-year-old daughter wander around the country?"

"I'm not wandering around the country, Mom. I'm delivering a horse, that's all."

She smoked a little more. Then I heard her start moving around fast like she does when she decides it's time to get going.

"You're doing this against my wishes, you understand that, Hattie?"

"Yes, Mom."

"This kind of behavior won't lead you any place you want to go. It's a bad start on your life."

"Mom, come on. Don't go overboard."

"I mean it. I don't know where we're heading with all this. You're more than I can handle."

"I'll be back by November at the latest, Mom. I'm going to apply for some jobs, and I promise I'll look into some community college courses. It will be okay."

"Just like that?"

"What do you want me to say, Mom?"

"I want to speak to Delores."

"She's inside in the bathroom," I lied. "We're at a rest stop."

"You tell her to give me a call tonight, then."

"I will."

"What should I tell the Fergusons?"

"Tell them I'm sorry. Tell them I didn't mean it as a whatever to them."

"A whatever?"

"What do you call it? A reproach?"

"Well, that's how they took it, young lady."

"I'll be back by November, Mom. Let's just leave it at that."

"You're lucky they're not calling the police on you. They like you, Hattie. They're very disappointed."

There was no answer to that, so I didn't say anything. Mom finally wound down. She said she loved me but I was really testing her. Pushing the envelope. Straining things. She said we needed to have a whole new way of going at things when I returned. A *whole* new way, she said, emphasizing the "whole." Then we hung up.

"How did it go?" Delores asked when she saw me finish.

"Great," I said, ladling on the sarcasm.

"She pissed?"

"Majorly."

"But she can't do anything, can she?"

"She wants to talk to you tonight."

"There's something to look forward to," Delores said. "You know what I'm learning? If you do what you want, most people can't do much about it. That's worth knowing."

She climbed in and started the truck.

"Let's find a spot to give Speed a break," I said. "He needs a good drink."

"Okay," she said.

"The Fergusons think we're being cruel to Speed. You think we are?"

"Anything is better than dead," Delores said, putting the truck in gear. "Almost, anyway."

WE SLIPPED OFF INTERSTATE 90 SOMEPLACE IN NEW YORK State and drove about twenty miles on back roads until we found a small rest stop that looked abandoned. Maybe once upon a time the rest stop sat on an active highway, but now it was grown over with weeds, and the pavement had buckled and broken in about a dozen places. Small picnic tables, with little roofs over them, dotted a grassy section. A creek about the size of a bowling alley ran through the middle of the area. A chipped sign at the western edge of the creek identified it as Blackeyed Creek.

We backed Speed out of the trailer and let him get his balance. He looked a little wobbly. We walked him down to the creek and took him in up to his shins. He drank a long, long time. Because it was warm out, we grabbed a sponge from the trailer and bathed him. The water perked him up. It was strange seeing him away from the Fergusons' stable. He looked better somehow, more of a horse, and we kept sponging him to watch the water roll off him. Afterward we took him to the grassy section and let him eat. He went at the grass right away, chewing with big yanks, one after another.

Delores grabbed some food we had thrown in a cooler—we had turkey cold cuts and white bread and a jar of mustard and one of mayo—and we fixed up two sandwiches. We filled our water bottles from the pump fountain next to the restrooms and added cherry powder. Then we sat for a while in the shade and watched Speed graze. He went for the clover first, sniffing it and eating it at the same time.

"Tell me about the bureau," Delores said, drinking from her water bottle.

"The Bureau of Land Management. 'The Wild Free-Roaming Horses and Burros Act of 1971, established to ensure that healthy herds thrive on healthy rangelands,'" I said, quoting the literature I had memorized.

"I like thinking about that. I like knowing it exists."

"You think Speed can survive on a rangeland?"

Delores shrugged. We both had our eyes on Speed. I knew Delores. She was coming to a low point. I could see the air going out of her. Sometimes she went so low that the only way back up was by breaking something. Sometimes the thing she broke was herself, and sometimes it was the people around her, and you couldn't head her off, couldn't chase her into a corner like you could a horse, because she couldn't think straight when she got like that. She was all nerve when she hit the bottom. It scared me when she headed that way, but it scared her more than anyone else. She said it felt like pond ice inside her, thin and ready to break, and underneath, miles of dark water waited, ready to gobble her up. She said she had once seen a duck frozen into a lake, its webbed feet trapped and glowing yellow under the ice, and that was the image that stayed with her. "Frozen duck," she said for shorthand when she got all turned around inside, and I hated to know that she saw that in her mind's eye.

"That's where I should go," she said, getting gritty in her eyes, "to the wild free-roaming rangeland for teenagers."

"'Thirty-three thousand horses roam Bureau of Land Management land in ten western states,'" I said, quoting again.

Then I looked at her closely.

"You okay?" I asked. "You getting major blue? You getting frozen duck?"

"No, I'm okay. Which state has the best rangeland?"

"Montana or Wyoming," I said, still watching her. "At least, I think so."

Delores didn't say anything for a little. When she spoke again, I knew she had been far away in her thoughts. Talking about horses and rangeland was only part of what she wanted.

"You think I should keep going?" she asked. "I mean, after?"

"I'd miss you."

"I'd miss you to the moon, too," she said. "But what do you think?"

"I don't know, Delores. It's different now that we're actually traveling. Your mom will break up with Larry soon. She always moves on."

"Larry," Delores said. "What a dimwit. Do you know what kind of car he drives? An El Camino. Part truck, part car. It's the freaking mullet of cars. Business up front, party at the back."

"You'll figure it out."

"You know," she said, "I think sometimes that the true reason we want Speed to get to the bureau land is so he won't live his whole life trapped and going in circles. Do you know what I mean? We're Speed. We're afraid we won't get to be horses."

"You're probably right," I said.

"And because Speed is about as nice a horse as ever lived."

"The gentlest. Will you call your mom?"

"Maybe later."

"Well, that will be awkward," I said, which was a gag phrase we used sometimes back and forth, but she didn't laugh or repeat it back.

When we finished our sandwiches, we went and hugged Speed. He allowed it, but mostly he wanted to eat the clover.

I DROVE IN THE AFTERNOON WHILE DELORES SLEPT. SHE looked pretty sleeping against the passenger window, her hair a little mussed, her knees tucked up for comfort. She was still asleep when we entered the tip of Pennsylvania, then Ohio. It felt strange driving on the interstate, flying along and taking miles under us. I wasn't strictly legal to drive. I had my license, but I could only drive with a person over twenty-five in the vehicle. Our plan was to switch seats fast if a cop pulled us over, and to keep it slow anyway. We figured cops didn't really want to stop a truck pulling a horse unless he or she absolutely had to.

I listened to some country-and-western station, soft and quiet. I drove, but I thought about Mom, and about home and bed, and about the Fergusons. Later I thought about the Przewalski's horse. I had done a report on them in ninth grade—the only wild horse left in the world. They lived in Mongolia, and they had never been domesticated. American mustangs and Australian brumbies were domestic horses that had gone feral. The same thing had happened to the wild burros and even some camels in the American West. Przewalski's horses roamed around the Mongolian plains the same way they had since the beginning of time. Then sometime in the 1960s they went extinct in the wild. That was the official designation. A few survived in zoos, and some good people set up a foundation, and they traded horse semen back and forth, and eventually they reintroduced a small herd of the Przewalski's horse back on the Mongolian steppes. The Przewalski's horse has sixty-six chromosomes, not sixty-four like domestic horses, which means they can crossbreed with donkeys or zebras and produce fertile offspring. It seemed to me that the Przewalski's horse was the Adam and Eve of horses, and maybe doing that report in ninth grade had led to my sitting behind the wheel of a Ford F-150 with a horse in the back, heading west.

That's what I was thinking when Delores woke up. Horse-crazy thoughts.

"WHERE ARE WE?" DELORES ASKED, PUSHING BACK HER hair and reaching for her water bottle.

"Ohio," I said.

"My mouth tastes like the back side of duct tape after you use it to clean the crumbs out of a couch in an elementary school for bed wetters," she said, starting a little game we played.

"Like," I said, "the fur on the paw of a dog walking across a cow pasture in the rain."

"Like," she said, "Jim Frank's armpits."

We both started laughing.

Jim Frank was the horrible band director we'd both had in our respective seventh grades. His shirt pits always gleamed yellow from sweat stains.

Delores wound down the passenger window.

"Getting colder," she said, sticking her hand out and cupping air toward her. "We should think about where we're going to sleep."

"I thought we were going to keep driving."

"I think maybe Speed needs a break. And we have time."

"Okay," I said.

"Just a couple hours, then we can buzz off."

"Someplace like that rest stop in New York State," I said.

"Or a farm," she said. "We should get off the interstate."

She pulled out her cell phone and checked the bars.

"I had it on mute. Three messages," she said. "All from Mommy Dearest."

She hit Messages and put the phone to her ear.

"Delores . . . ," she said, repeating some of the words her mother used, and grinning at me. "Delores . . . big mistake . . . reckless . . . cousin Richard's trailer . . . truck . . . bad. Bad, bad, bad. Delores . . . right away . . . that horse is going to . . . if anything happens . . . I mean it . . . since you were a girl . . . Larry. Yes, Larry . . ."

She hung up.

"Well," she said. "That was awkward."

We both laughed. Delores reached for the radio and cranked it high. We screamed our guts out to Faith Hill's "This Kiss." Wind blowing in, crisp air, Ohio.

"IT'S ME. DELORES."

Delores held the phone away from her ear. I heard her mom yelling on the other end.

When her mom stopped yelling, Delores put the phone to her ear again.

"Delores is not here," Delores said, lowering her voice into a growl. "I am Satan and I have taken her soul."

More yelling. Delores gave me a big grin.

"Nice talking to you, Mom," Delores said when her mom stopped yelling.

She hung up.

One second later the phone rang.

"This is Satan," Delores said. "May I ask who's calling?"

A quick burst of yelling.

"What do you want me to say, Mom?" Delores asked finally. "If you just want to yell at me, okay. Yell away. But if you think I'll take that seriously, you're dreaming."

Her mother spoke for a long time. Delores's grin fell off her face in little chunks. She listened. I looked over as much as I could. I put my hand on her knee and rubbed it.

"I'm sorry you feel that way, Mom," Delores said after a time. "I'm sorry for everything. We'll get the trailer back to cousin Richard. . . . Yes. Hattie is coming back. . . . Right. I don't know. Maybe."

Delores hung up.

I reached over and grabbed her hand. She squeezed it. Then she looked away to the window.

"She's debating calling the cops on us, but that's a bluff, because she doesn't want the cops sniffing around her any more than I do. I'm not welcome back home. I'm now officially invited to stay gone. She wanted me to know that. What else is new?"

"You okay?"

"Sure," she said. "Swell. She said that all my life I've been screwing up. She said she can't have me in the house as a model for Sissy."

"Like Sissy needs any help being Sissy," I said.

Sissy was her little sister and a little hellion.

"And," Delores said, "she doesn't think twice about hooking up with Larry, bringing him home, letting him hang around with his nasty tattoos and his looks. I saw him looking at Sissy the other day and it was just disgusting."

I didn't say anything.

"You know what I would like?" Delores said after a while. "I'd like a campfire. Just a fire. Maybe we could find a campground and build a little fire. We could let Speed out of the trailer for the night so he could stretch his legs."

I nodded and said, "We could do that."

We drove. Delores leaned her head against the passenger window. We still held hands.

"Where am I supposed to go, anyway?" she asked. "Where does she expect me to go?"

"It's okay, sweetie. We'll figure it out."

"You know, when I tried that . . . ," she said, and pointed at her wrists, "she never told Sissy. She said Sissy didn't need to know her sister was crazy. She told me I was her first try and that Sissy was her second try and you always got the second try to turn out better."

Delores's face crumpled then. She turned to the window and cried. I held her hand. I searched around inside my head for something to say, but I didn't have any good words for her. She was right about her situation. Her mom wanted Larry to take a bigger slice. She called him the Larinator, and twice she had markered tattoos on her arm, practicing for the real one she wanted to get to represent their love. Delores's mother liked to say she had put eighteen years into Delores and wasn't seeing any kind of return on her investment so she wasn't throwing good money after bad. Larry, she said, would be different. Larry knew how to treat a woman, her mom said, which was a laugh to everyone in the world except to her mom.

We drove along the top of Ohio. The horse trailer rocked nice and easy behind us.

Chapter 3

WE FOLLOWED MEL CLEMENS THROUGH A MAZE OF campers and RVs. He drove an electric golf cart. He wore a navy Windbreaker and a white visor. He had to be close to eighty. His office had about a dozen plaques saying things about life being golf, or golf is life. You had the feeling he was trying to talk himself into believing it. But he had been nice and friendly, and he had been willing to give us a site where we could tether Speed and have a fire, too. The camping fee was twenty-two dollars and included showers.

Our lights snapped against tent walls and camper sides, and twice we entered a short stretch of forest. Moths clicked through our headlights. Delores drove and leaned forward to see better. Finally Mel Clemens gave us an arm wave to turn in left. Trees lined the left side of the site, but the right side opened onto pasture that had turned quiet and frosty under the large moon.

"You girls should do okay here," Mel said, climbing out of his golf cart and joining us in the headlight beams. "Your horse can eat all he wants in this meadow. Can't do any harm at all. You can burn that bundle of wood we threw into your truck, but you can burn just about anything you find on the ground around here. This site is a little overrun. Sorry, but it's a good spot for the horse."

"It'll do just fine," Delores said.

"Long way to the bathhouse, but again, I took the horse into consideration."

"Perfect," I said.

"We have seventy-two slots here. Of course, with the economy the way it's going, some of them are taken full-time. Month by month, I mean. We don't get many girls traveling alone."

"We're not alone. We have a horse," Delores said.

Mel smiled but didn't seem to mean it.

"It's getting a little cold," Delores said. "Guess we'll get that fire going."

"Well, you know where to find us if you need anything. Quiet hours are from ten on. No liquor, no drugs."

We both nodded.

"Okay, then," Mel said. "Sleep tight."

He climbed back into his cart, backed it around once, then took off with a wave.

"It's dark," Delores said when he was gone.

"We've got headlamps."

"Let's get Speed out."

We backed Speed out of the trailer. He came slowly, looking a little tired and unsure of his footing in the darkness. We slipped a long lead on him and tied it to the handle of the truck. He found some grass and started eating. I filled up a rubberized water bucket from the spigot near the campfire ring and waddled over with it. Speed took a good long drink. I stayed awhile and rubbed his neck while Delores started making a fire. I whispered that he was a pretty boy, the prettiest I had ever seen. Then I put my forehead against his neck and breathed him inside me. It made my heart hurt to feel how much I loved him.

"Get twigs," Delores said when I finished with Speed.

She had a tiny fire going. She had used a piece of road map as starter.

I collected wood in the small forest to our left. I searched for dry stuff and eventually found a downed pine tree. I snapped off branches and twigs and hurried back. The fire had nearly died, but the pine revived it. Delores put the pine in carefully, letting the flame swing from one twig to the next.

"Now, that's better," Delores said when we finally had a solid flame. "My grandfather used to say the whole world becomes a fire wherever you build one."

"It's getting colder," I said, my hands out to the flames. "I can feel it on my back."

"I think we're south of where we started."

"Still," I said.

"Let's pull the picnic table closer."

We did. Then we sat. Everything was dark except for the fire. We added a few pieces of wood we had purchased from Mel. They hissed. I fed some pine in to give them life.

"Speed is having an adventure," I said, my hands out to the fire. "You think this is the farthest west he's ever been?"

"Probably. Didn't the Fergusons say he had come from western Massachusetts?"

"A pony riding place."

"Then the Humane Society took him?"

"Only when the place closed down. The owners had

nowhere to house the horses. And they had no money for food. Speed wasn't in good shape when the Fergusons got him. I was there the day he came. I fell in love with him the minute I saw him back out of the trailer. He was dignified, Delores. You could see he was tired and probably badly fed, but he didn't expect any special kindness. He kills me. I don't know why, but he does."

"I'll give them that, then," Delores said. "Taking Speed in, I mean."

"They're nice people," I said. "They are."

"They like you, for some reason. Not that you're not likeable. But they've taken an interest in you, I guess is what I'm saying. They never quite knew what to do with me when I came around the stable to visit you."

"Well, they won't think much of me after this."

"You never know. They might respect you for it if they're as horse crazy as you say they are. Write it off as a young person's inexperience."

"The whole thing seems pretty straightforward to me. We're just giving a horse a different perspective."

"You're a dreamer, Hattie," Delores said.

We ate three quarters of a bag of marshmallows Delores had purchased with the wood. Now and then the light from the fire shrugged higher with a breeze and we caught little snapshots of Speed grazing contentedly, his bulk glistening. Delores's grandfather had been correct: the whole world had become our fire. We sat and ate and licked our fingers. Delores insisted on roasting a marshmallow once, peeling and eating it, then roasting it again. She called it CPR, the char, peel, repeat system. Like getting two marshmallows for one, she said.

We were still eating when the four-wheelers came.

We heard them a long way off and didn't think much of them. Then they came closer and we saw Speed's head jerk up. What had been mere engine sound and glaring headlights a moment before materialized as four ATVs screeching into a half circle around us.

We couldn't see a thing. The lights blinded us. The revving engines made Speed take a few steps away, his ears upraised and turning to understand what had invaded his grazing.

"Don't act scared," Delores whispered to me. "Just keep eating."

I did. We did. The ATVs idled and kept their lights on us. It was clear they wanted to taunt us. Maybe they had seen us come into the campground. Maybe this was their way to fight their own stupid boredom.

Suddenly Delores stood and threw her marshmallow stick at the ATVs.

"Get out of here!" she shouted. "Who asked you to come around?"

They backed off. Then one of the drivers, being funny, revved forward like he was going to ride right through our camp. I suspected they were young guys—idiot boys—but I couldn't tell for sure with their helmets and everything. They might have been aliens, for all I could see. Delores picked up a rock and held it above her head. She didn't say anything. Finally the ATV on the right peeled away and headed back toward the center of the campground. The others followed. The one who had revved his engine did it some more as he gunned off. Teasing us.

"What wicked wheeze bags," Delores said when they had finally pulled away. "I hate those things."

"Who were they?" I asked, feeling sick and dizzy from the fumes and the fright and the marshmallows.

"Just jerks," Delores said. "Dumb boys who think because they ride an ATV they amount to something."

"Give me a horse any day," I said.

I went and settled Speed. I made sure his lead moved freely across the ground. And I grabbed a blanket out of the trailer and draped it over his shoulders. He nickered a little when I rubbed his forehead. He put his head up and let me balance it on my shoulder. He smelled of horse and barn and grass. I loved his smell and told him so.

Delores came over and petted Speed, too. We fussed over him. Mostly we used him to get our courage warmed up.

"You think they'll come back?" I asked.

"The ATV jerks? They better not."

"What did they want, anyway?"

"They wanted our magnificence."

"Seriously," I said.

"Get a rise out of us, that's all. They're bored. They feel tough on the ATVs. It's a boy thing."

"You think they might have mistaken us for someone they knew?"

"They thought we were a Burger King, Hattie," Delores said. "You're too trusting for your own good."

We talked about the ATVs until the fire ran out of fuel and we had stuffed ourselves with marshmallows. Yawning, we laid out our sleeping bags on the hood of the truck and put our backs against the windshield. The engine still sent a bit of warmth through the hood, and it felt good to absorb it and look up at the stars. The sky hung low and clean.

"This is the farthest west I've been," I said, referring back to our conversation about Speed.

"I went once with my dad to Colorado. He drove a truck out there for a friend. I don't remember much. I was pretty little."

"Where is your dad, Delores?"

"Last we heard he was in Oregon."

"You ever think about trying to track him down?"

"Only every day."

"What was he like?"

"He was short, actually. Kind of a small guy, and wiry. Mom always called him the Jockey when she got mad at him. Redheaded, kind of, but the brown kind of redhead, not the orange kind."

"You've got his coloring. Your coloring is pretty. My mom says you look British."

She waved at a mosquito.

"He did tree work," Delores said, intent on her own thoughts, "for a logging company, topping off big trees, until a landscaper hired him to down dead trees on expensive properties. That kind of thing. But he skipped out of work a lot. He didn't drink or anything, he just lost interest. Then he drifted away, taking longer and longer trips on errands or doing things like bringing that truck to Colorado. One day the kite string broke. That's what Mom said."

"You think your mom still loves him?"

"She says loving anyone after this long is loving a ghost. He left when I was about eight, I think. Mom says you don't really remember who that person is or was, you just remember a murky image. She's probably right about that."

A bat cut through the stars for a second. It erased the stars, flicking back and forth, taking the light of the stars on its wings. We watched in silence.

"How about you?" Delores said. "You hear from your dad much?"

"Now and then. He sends Mom some support money sometimes, but it doesn't really get to me directly. It was court mandated for household accounts."

"Where is he?"

"Maryland. He's got another family down there. He does okay, I guess. Drywalling."

"Everyone needs drywall."

"You're poking fun, but it's true."

"Why did they split up, anyway?"

"Erosion, Mom says. They just wore each other to sand."

"You think you want to get married and do all that?" Delores asked. "The kids, the house, the whole deal? I mean, given our parents' track record, you think it even makes sense to try it?"

"I'm not sure," I sighed. "Trying it seems like a normal thing, but when you think about it, there's nothing sensible about trying to live with someone."

"And boys are crazy," Delores said. "Just crazy."

"I've never really dated anyone. It seems kind of confusing to me. You dated that guy Eugene, right?"

"He was my lover man, Hattie," Delores said, and bumped her shoulder into mine. She almost made me slide off the hood. But I knew her history. She had been crazy for Eugene for about three days. Then she cooled like a lava flow. She became all rock, all pumice, with bright holes in her surface, as though the heat had been too much. She never even gave Eugene a reason for breaking up. She just trapped him in her heat, like the people in a village at the foot of a volcano, and he looked charred and stunned for weeks afterward.

We lay against the windshield without speaking. In the quiet, we heard a tiny brook running somewhere in the forest. Cold air moved over the campsite, and the fire glowed red. I played with the image of the red fire, clicking my eyes back and forth and turning it into an eye of a dragon lying flat on the ground and looking up, then into the top of a volcano on a midget island where no one grew taller than four feet and the biggest houses only came up to your waist. That was the kind of thing I thought about when my mind washed around. That shift of mind hurt me in school a lot. Teachers usually wrote home and said I was dreamy or a woolgatherer. They were probably right, but I liked chasing my own thoughts. I always had.

We dozed and fell asleep. I woke twice to listen for Speed. Once I heard him chewing, and another time I heard his lead knock against his water barrel. I imagined climbing onto his back and feeling his wings sprout from his shoulders and great rays of light coming out of the sky to pull him home. All horses become Pegasus at the moment of their death. That's what my first riding teacher told me, and that's what I believed.

Delores's phone woke us.

It rang and rang and eventually Delores slid off the hood and pawed through the truck cab until she came up with the phone. The sun hadn't fully shaken free of the land. It still peppered through mist and fog and everything looked gray and quiet. Speed had settled on his stomach, but the sound of the phone brought him up onto his feet. He took his time getting there. He moved like an old man.

"What?" Delores said into the phone. "What are you saying?"

I slid off the truck hood. I felt stiff and lumpy. I folded the two sleeping bags and put them in the truck. Then I found a few more pine twigs and put them into the smoking ashes from the night before. I blew on them and they caught easily. I built the fire while Delores talked into the phone. She slid into the truck cab eventually and leaned her head back against the window, listening.

When I had the fire solid again, I worked Speed over with a rubber curry brush. I concentrated on his sides and hips, where dirt had worked its way under his hair. When I finished with that, I used a dandy brush on him to get the last of the dirt. He took it without complaint. It was a good moment, actually, with Speed. The air came fresh through the meadow and forest, and the sound of the fire behind us made it cheerful. I brushed him quietly and he leaned a little into me. I lost myself in my hands, let them do whatever they wanted, because having a horse in my care made more sense than anything else I could think about. A horse lives in the present, right now, right this minute, and when I moved my hands over Speed, I felt quiet and calm inside. I finished by giving him a couple carrots, and he took them with a big nod each time I let him nibble one into his mouth.

"That was Larry," Delores said when I went back to the fire. She had plopped down on the picnic table. Her hair looked wild and uncombed. She had fed the fire a little higher, and it burned easily, cracking the mist that rolled around at our feet.

"What did Larry want?"

"Oh, he tried to be all fatherly for me. Mom put him up to it. How am I supposed to listen to a guy with an El Camino and a mullet?"

"Awkward," I said, sitting next to her on the picnic table.

"I want pancakes," she said.

"We can get pancakes. You okay?"

"Larry said they talked it over and he'd volunteered to call because maybe I'd be calmer with him. You know, like he's Mr. United Nations or something."

"Why so early?"

"They figured they would get me that way. I looked at the number and almost didn't answer, but then I wondered if something important had happened."

"So, what was his advice?"

"He didn't have any, really. He called to say they had decided to try to get in touch with my father. They thought maybe I should go live with him a little if they can track him down."

"In Oregon?"

She nodded.

"Well," I said. "Least that's not as lame as it could have been, right?"

"It's pretty lame. He doesn't want me out there. He hasn't been in touch for ten years or whatever."

"Can't hurt to try."

"The definition of 'crazy' is someone who presses button A ten times, gets response B ten times, but keeps pressing A expecting a different result."

"You're pretty philosophical this morning."

"I'm an extremely deep thinker," she said, and grinned.

We sat and watched the fire for a while. The temperature felt to be in the forties somewhere. I had the kind of cold face and crusty eyes you get from sleeping outdoors.

"How many marshmallows did we eat last night, anyway?" Delores asked.

"About a million."

"We ate a whole bag. We're a pair of Hog-a-thas."

"We fed a couple to Speed. And we dropped a couple in the fire."

"How about those idiot boys on ATVs? What was their deal?"

"Testosterone," I said.

"What is that, anyway? Girls would never circle a bunch of boys on ATVs and sit there gunning their engines. It just wouldn't happen."

Delores shrugged.

"I want warm food," she said, pushing up and blowing her nose on a tissue she had in her pocket. She chucked it onto the fire. "Let's get rolling."

DELORES HAD THE HEAT BLASTING—WE WERE COLD—AND everything was just getting settled on the way out of the campground, when we saw the ATVs. Four of them, all Hondas. I knew at a glance that they were *our* ATVs, the ones driven by the jerk boys. I recognized two of the helmets sitting out on the picnic table.

Delores looked at me and slowed. She got her crazy-evil look and wiggled her eyebrows.

She slowly eased her truck up to the first ATV. She put the nose of the truck right against it, then gently ladled the engine forward. The ATV skidded slowly sideways, directly into the second ATV. She goosed the engine a little more, and both ATVs skidded and chucked sideways, tipping and bouncing. I heard some crashing and breaking things, and suddenly two boys shot out of a big tent, both of them in hoodies and boxers.

"Hey!" they yelled, but they couldn't do anything. They ran back and forth, looking at the damage and yelling at us.

Delores stuck her tongue at them. I did, too.

Then Delores backed up and swung the nose of the truck away and laid on the horn. The horn was shockingly loud in the early morning.

"Do not ever, ever, ever screw around with a woman going west," Delores shouted.

My mom called Delores's cell phone at breakfast. Delores read the number and handed it to me and made a funny grimace.

"Indiana," I said when she asked where we were. "I think, anyway."

"You don't even know the state?"

"Indiana."

"Where did you spend last night?"

"At a campground. It was fine, Mom."

"I'm just sick with fear for you two. Delores was supposed to call me last night."

"We can take care of ourselves," I said, letting Delores's failure to call go without comment. Sometimes my mom forgot to come back to things if I changed the subject. "I have to eat now. The waitress brought the food just this minute."

"She did not."

"Yes, she did, Mom."

"I don't get what the point of this is. Can you explain what in the world you're doing, Hattie?"

"We're women going west," I said.

"What is that, like a catchphrase?"

"It's a statement of fact."

We didn't speak for a moment. Delores slipped out of the booth and headed toward the ladies' room.

"Mom, didn't you ever just want to do something because you thought you should do it?"

She didn't answer.

"I love Speed, Mom. I love him more than anything. I want him to be a horse for just one minute of his life. That's all. Then I'll come home."

"Couldn't he be a horse in New Hampshire?"

"I want to put him on rangeland. Imagine your whole life you've gone in circles. Imagine what that must be like."

"I feel like I have, almost," she said. "I think I know."

"Speed has. If he hits a trail that goes left, he takes it. His whole body knows how to do only one thing. It's pitiful."

"But he can't live on the range. The Fergusons said that was out of the question."

"It probably is. But I want to give him a chance."

"You are too horse crazy for your own good."

"And Delores has to go west. Her mom is trying to get in touch with her dad in Oregon."

"Delores is not your responsibility. Delores has her own issues, Hattie. I'm sorry to say it, but she does."

"I know."

"I spoke to the Fergusons and they said they have friends with land in Montana. They said you could bring Speed there if you wanted."

"He'll be okay," I said.

"I hope so. I hope you'll be okay."

"I've got to go," I said. "We're having pancakes."

"You always liked pancakes."

"And always will."

Chapter 4

DELORES TOLD ME A HUNDRED TIMES WHICH STATE WAS
which, but I couldn't get Ohio, Indiana, and Illinois straightened out. The signs over the highways changed, and some of
the road surfaces varied, but it was all just concrete and light
stanchions and cars whizzing everywhere. Delores said the
roads were modern rivers, and that populations grew around
them just the way they did back in the day when rivers carried
most of the country's goods, but I didn't care for her analogy.

Late in the afternoon we passed through Chicago. We
both sat up to look around, but the traffic moved so slowly
that we worried about Speed. Then it started to mist, and we
figured that was a relief to Speed. I had the map spread on

my lap. Delores said right around the bend from Chicago we could get to Wisconsin, then Minnesota. A friend of hers had told her that the sky opened up once you passed Blue Earth, Minnesota. That the West began in Blue Earth.

"Does Chicago look like Chicago?" Delores asked when we had assured ourselves we followed the proper route. "I mean, there should be a word for a thing that doesn't look like you thought a thing should look."

"How about 'disappointment'?"

"Naw," Delores said.

"What's Chicago supposed to look like, anyway? All cities look the same when you drive past them."

"The Bible says if you live among the masses, you'll die among the masses."

"Well, that's awkward."

On the northern outskirts of Chicago, still in traffic, we tuned in to Dr. Black, a radio psychiatrist who helped people with personal problems. Someone would call in with a complaint about their husband—he had been cheating, or his cell phone had another woman's number on it—and we tried to prescribe the proper response before the doctor weighed in on the question. Delores was wicked good at it. Whenever a woman had a man problem, she would yell, "Kick him to the curb, sister," but then she got a serious look on her face and tried to sort things through. She nodded as she spoke. As soon as we heard the whole problem, we turned down the volume on the radio and played at being Dr. Black.

Mostly women called in with problems about men and children. Sometimes men called in and asked how to get a woman back after she had stormed out. Families caused their share of problems, too. A dozen calls came in about mean mothers-in-law, or fathers who needed to stop driving because of dementia, or an adolescent boy who wanted to get a tattoo.

"I'd like to be a psychologist," Delores said during a commercial. "You sit and listen to everyone's problems and try to guide them. They can't get mad if it doesn't work, because they're screwed up to begin with."

"You'd be like a dump for them, though. They'd chuck everything at you. It wouldn't be pretty."

"You might feel better knowing your life doesn't stink as bad as you thought it did. And they get paid pretty well, right?"

"You'd be good at it," I said.

"You know," Delores said, "I once watched an old *Twilight Zone* about a sin-eater. This guy would go to funerals, and the grieving families would lay out a big meal that no one but the sin-eater could touch. Really beautiful food back when they didn't have great food. And the sin-eater would sit in front of it, and I think a priest would say something. I don't remember that part so well."

"Then what?"

"Then the sin-eater would eat the food. He'd just shove it into his mouth like crazy, and he'd be gurgling and crying because he was eating the dead man's sins, too. That was the only way the dead guy would get to heaven. So then the sin-eater would collapse, but not before shoving food into his coat pockets to bring home to his family. It went on like that for a lot of years until one day the sin-eater himself died."

"Well, what did people do?" I asked, still looking out at the city.

"They starved the daughter of the sin-eater's family. Then one day they opened the door to a spare room, and the sin-eater's body was in there surrounded by food. The girl tried to resist, but her mother kept whispering, 'Go ahead, eat it, go ahead, your father needs to go to heaven.'"

"Did she eat the food?"

"I'm not telling."

"You are, too," I said.

Then Chicago ended and I had to get money for a toll.

We entered Wisconsin and saw a guy driving a truck with a cheese triangle on his head.

We stopped for hay at a feed store in Caseyville, somewhere between Sparta and Onalaska. Two old men sat on a porch outside the store. One of them smoked a cigar. I couldn't blame them for wanting to be outside. The day had turned soft and warm, and the sun felt strong. A blond cat sat perched on the railing in front of the men. We were ten miles off the interstate at least.

"Hay's around back, if that's what you're looking for," one of the men said. "Just pay Julie inside."

We thanked him.

Julie turned out to be at least as old as the men. She was tall and well kept, with white hair pulled back in a spray behind her ears. She wore crisp jeans and a bright flannel shirt that had faded to white in spots. A pencil jabbed through her hair. She had a ledger book open in front of her and a pair of bifocals propped on her nose.

"We'd like four bales of hay, please," Delores said.

"First cut is five seventy-five a bale," Julie said, hardly looking up.

I fished the money out of my jeans. I put down twenty-five

dollars. Julie made change and slid the money back to me. She smelled like lavender.

"Can you pull around back?" Julie asked, slipping out of a pair of moccasins and sliding into a pair of muck boots. "I'll meet you there."

We went out.

"New Hampshire?" one of the men said, reading our license plate. "You're a long way from home."

"Looks like it," I said.

"You bringing a horse to someone?"

I nodded.

"Never been to New Hampshire," the man said. "Farthest east I ever ventured is New York State. Went to the Adirondacks. Pretty nice country, a lot like Wisconsin."

"New Hampshire is pretty," I said. "Cold and pretty."

We got back into the truck and pulled around behind the store. Julie waved us to a tent where she stored the hay.

"You girls from New Hampshire?" Julie asked.

"Yes, ma'am," Delores said.

"I grew up in New Hampshire. Until I was five. You ever hear of a place called Rumney?"

"That's where we're from," I said. "Next town over."

"Small world," Julie said, and looked at us more closely. "My father worked on a train line there. Milk train. They used to bring the milk into Boston in the afternoon. Then trucks became the order of the day and they got rid of the trains. That was a darn shame, I promise you. Dad moved us west. He always did like cows. This is all dairy country around here."

She pulled open a plastic flap and showed us the hay.

"You girls are younger than I am," she said. "Just step inside and grab four bales. You're welcome to any loose hay if you want to sweep it up. It gets thrown around in here when people pull out bales."

We stuck our hands into the bales to check them for heat or mold. If you feed a horse wet or rotted hay, you open yourself up to colic; if it's too dusty, you can cause respiratory problems. Julie watched us.

"You girls know what you're doing," she said, approving. "But that's good hay. We get it local."

"Smells good," Delores said.

"Oh, one of the best smells on earth, if you like horses. I come back here sometimes and eat my lunch sitting near it. I used to keep horses years ago. Of course, I can't quite ride anymore. Too much up and down for these old bones. But once you like horses, you can't get them out of your head."

We fit the hay under a tarp in the rear of the truck. Julie walked back to take a look at Speed. I scooped up a couple armfuls of hay and pushed it through to Speed. He looked asleep.

"An old horse like that, you ought to put him to pasture for a day," Julie said, her hand reaching in to pet Speed. "Let him catch up to himself. Have you been driving straight through?"

"We took a break last night," I said.

"You can't rush an old horse. Are you going far?"

"Wyoming," I said.

Julie nodded.

"You feed him any alfalfa pellets? Any concentrates?"

"Mostly hay and pasture," I said.

"We have some feeds with some aspirin in it now. Might be good for his joints."

"We'll keep that in mind," Delores said.

Julie pulled her hand out and stuck it into the back pocket of her pants. She smiled. One of her front teeth lay slightly across the other front tooth, leaning to the left. She had good lines around her eyes. Happy lines. She had the ghost of a long laugh in her face.

"I know you're thinking I'm a crazy, meddlesome woman, but there's a stable out back here. And a pasture loaded with clover, all fenced. You're more than welcome to turn him out on it for a while. Spend the night if you like. I'd hate to see him overtaxed by the trip."

I looked at Delores. She shrugged. We had one of those moments when we couldn't quite read the other person. It was hard to know what to do. Maybe the woman was nuts, but she didn't seem like it. And maybe she and the men out front would grab us and lock us in the cellar and make us eat chicken hearts. Delores and I could usually get around most things, but a straight-out offer proved trickier.

"If you're sure we wouldn't be in the way," I said, trying to read Delores and figuring we could change our minds later if we didn't want to stay.

"We had the stables for our horses, and they haven't been used in a couple years. But we keep them up just in case. Those two old crows you saw sitting on the porch, they like a project now and then, so I send them back here to putz around. Water is hooked right there from that faucet. What's the horse's name, anyway?"

"Speed," I said.

"If he's as old as I think he is, you ought to give him a break. Tomorrow's another day. He'll be stronger for a rest. They sweat a lot of water in these trailers. Just no fires. Promise me that. Town's not far away, so you can run in there for a pizza or something. No one will bother you. No one will even know you're out here except for me and my husband, Jack. Our house is just an eighth of a mile down."

She examined us closely.

"You're not into drugs or any of that stuff, are you?"

"No," Delores said, stretching things like she does when she pretends to speak French, "we're straight-edge."

"What in the world is that?"

"We keep our senses pure. It's kind of a way."

Julie shook her head.

"What are your names, anyway?"

We introduced ourselves.

"I'd no more trust anyone who is straight-edge than I'd trust a born-again Christian," Julie said. "Life's more rounded than straight-edged. Just don't do any drugs out here and don't bring any boys out from town after you. That's the deal."

I nodded. Delores shook hands with Julie.

"Should be a good moon," Julie said. "Mind if I help you off-load Speed? It's been a while since I've handled a horse."

"Sure," I said.

Julie put her hand up to silence us.

"Jack!" she yelled. "You got the store."

She waited.

"Jack!" she yelled again. "You got the store."

A soft voice answered, "Okay."

"A man always hears the first time," Julie said, smiling at us, "but he makes you tell him twice. Especially if he's your husband. Men have their tricks. Don't ever think they don't. Now just bring your truck through and we can put Speed right in the middle of the pasture. He'll have a nice night there, and you two can use a break, I bet. Wait till Jack hears we have a horse out back. He'll flip."

WE SET UP THE TENT ON A FLAT PIECE OF MEADOW NOT FAR from the sheep fence that corralled the pasture. It was an L.L.Bean Eureka two-person tent, green, with good zippers and a tight fly. The grass folded down under it so that when we slid in to try it out, the sleeping bags felt fluffy and soft. I could have fallen asleep on the spot, but Delores dragged me out and made me promise we'd go into town.

We had a moment then. It snuck in on us, because that part of Wisconsin was not anyone's idea of a postcard. But the sun lay about two fingers off the horizon, and it cut down hard and soft at the same time, reminding you of summer and autumn both, and it picked up old Speed and turned him large and shadowy and pure. His silhouette stretched almost across the pasture, and he moved along eating, his tail flicking at late flies, and each step he took you heard through the ground. It was something old and pretty, back in the day of horses, and I had this romantic idea that someday I would have horses, and a house off a meadow, and we would have good, clean water for the animals and a wide porch where we could sit and watch them. It wasn't this place. This was just the back lot of a store, but it had the suggestion of something better, kinder, and I knew we both sensed it, Delores and me. Speed looked beautiful and calm, and I was glad Julie talked us into stopping. And the tent waited, soft and sweet, and tonight we would sleep comfortably, and Speed would be free under a big moon to feel his heart leaning west.

"Pretty here," Delores said, seeing it all, too.

"Sure is."

"She's a crazy old lady."

"She likes horses, is all," I said. "We'd be like that if we saw two girls going along. I mean, if we were old ladies and saw them."

"I guess so," Delores agreed.

"Women going west," I said. "That's what we are."

"She was funny about her husband. Come on, let's go get a pizza."

It was no big deal to weave our way back out to the main

highway and turn left. Delores switched on some country music, and we drove with the windows down. I liked that feeling right then. We felt good and tired and headed toward a decent meal. A sign told us town rested six miles away. We drove slow and easy. I held my hand out and let the wind tug it up and down.

The phone rang. It surprised us both because we had figured we were out of range. I picked it up, looked at the caller ID, and mouthed to Delores it was from our friend Paulette. I showed the phone to Delores and raised my eyebrows to ask if I should answer it. Before Delores responded, the phone cut out. Then it rang again.

"Do I answer it?" I asked.

Delores shrugged. "Whatever."

"Hello," I said.

"Hattie? Is that you? Where in the world are you two?"

It was Paulette.

"Wisconsin," I said.

"You guys just took off!" she yelled, her voice going up on the last word. "I am *soooooo* jealous."

"We took Speed to give him a vacation," I said.

"I know! Your parents have been trying to find out where you are. They called the cops!"

"Who did?"

Delores looked at me. She slowed the truck.

"I don't know all the details, but Delores's mom called over here. So did your dad—or, no, Delores's dad. I didn't even know she had a dad."

"Your dad called," I whispered to Delores, covering the mouthpiece of the phone.

"What?" Delores asked, her brows knitting. But Paulette went on talking.

"I guess Delores's mom called him and said you were heading west. He had a big tizz and threatened to call the police. Her cousin Richard, too, he wanted to call the police because you have some sort of van or trailer. I would have covered for you two, but I didn't know!"

"We didn't want to get you involved," I said. "We didn't tell anyone. That way no one can be blamed."

"Okay, I won't let it hurt my feelings, but I am jealous. Really jealous. It's so dull here. You wouldn't believe how dull."

"What did Delores's dad say?" I asked.

"He asked if I knew where you were. I said no, I didn't even know about this. He called it a caper. Can you believe it? Someone actually called it a caper. I guess he's up in arms. Delores's mom called my mom, and your mom is in it, too,

Hattie. I couldn't sort it all out. I've been trying to call you for two days, but you don't pick up."

"Sorry," I said. "We've been turning the phone off. And we've been out of range a lot. We don't check messages on purpose."

"I don't blame you, now that I know what's going on. You guys are crazy!"

"What about the cops?"

"I'm not sure. I don't know if it was for real or not. Delores's dad said she had taken a minor across a state line and that was against the law. He sounded like a dink. Don't tell Delores I said that, though."

"She doesn't really know him."

"I guess her mom is upset at his reaction. All heavy-handed and everything. She just called to let him know you might be heading out that way. Then he became all Mr. Parent and started wigging out on everyone. He called Delores's mom irresponsible. Then Larry got involved and told him to stay off the phone if that was the way he was going to talk. You know, that chest-to-chest stuff."

"What?" Delores said. "Tell me."

She pulled over and I gave her the phone. We switched places. She made Paulette repeat everything. She held one finger in her left ear and kept the phone pressed close to her right. I more or less knew how the conversation went by the questions she asked. Paulette's voice sounded like a high, excited insect on the other end.

Delores thanked Paulette and hung up as we entered the outskirts of town.

"It's official," Delores said, "we're criminals."

"Your dad?"

"I can't believe it."

"And now he's the daddest of dads."

"I know. Superdad. It's too freaking weird."

"Do you think the cops are actually after us?"

"The cops? Who knows? We're not hard to spot. A horse trailer and New Hampshire plates in Wisconsin. We'd better play it like they're after us anyway."

"You think they'll shoot us?"

"It's serious, Hattie."

"We'll stay on back roads."

"We're going to have to," Delores said. "We don't have a choice."

"We should have told Paulette to find out more information. She should be our spy."

"I'm still trying to get over the fact that my dad's involved. Or even that my mom knew how to get in touch with him."

She suddenly got up on her knees and stuck her head out the window. She yelled into the wind coming past, letting out some noise she had inside her. A kid on a bike turned to look at us. He nodded. Delores slid back inside. She shook her head.

"Pig spit," she said.

"We're in it now."

"This is awkward," Delores said.

We both started laughing. I'm not sure why. But we kept laughing. Delores said something about Larry coming to get us in his El Camino, and that became an image, Larry roaring west, his mullet waving in the breeze, the vehicle, half truck, half car, Johnny Cash on the radio, only Johnny Cash, and Larry would be decked out in black and silver, with boots and spurs, and Delores's dad would start from the other side of the country, and they would have a showdown, a square-off right in Wisconsin or Minnesota. We kept adding to the absurdity of it, and that made us laugh harder. Then we talked about how it must have sounded to her dad. He hadn't heard word one about his kid in a decade and then he gets a phone call to tell him she's heading across the country in his direction.

By the time we finished with all that, I had parked outside of Frand's Hardware & Paint store. We climbed out and stood

for a second, stretching. A raised walk fronted the stores. A toy railroad town, I thought. A town that had climbed onto a train and left about fifty years ago, leaving bones behind.

"I want to get some nail polish," Delores said, spotting an open drugstore. "We can ask inside about pizza."

We crossed the street and went inside. The drugstore smelled like cotton swabs and hair spray. Delores wandered the aisles until she found a polish display. She selected a bottle called Ruby Red Party. She held it next to her face and squinted in the mirror. She said it picked up her skin tone.

We paid and asked a young girl at the counter where we could get a pizza.

"Down the block," she said, pointing north.

"Is it good?"

The girl shrugged. As she did, Delores's phone rang again.

DELORES DIDN'T RECOGNIZE THE NUMBER, AND SHE refused to answer it.

"It could be Larry," she said. "Or my dad. Too freaky either way."

"Maybe we shouldn't answer the phone anymore."

"Maybe." She slipped the phone into her back pocket.

"Let's get pizza," she said.

We ordered a half pepperoni, half mushroom pie from a tall, greasy-looking boy who wore a white chef's cap and a striped shirt. I could tell it made him nervous to have two girls talking to him. Delores grabbed two orange sodas and a bunch of napkins, and we sat at a white plastic table near the window. We were the only customers. We sat and watched the sun disappear. It cast a reflection on a window across the street and burned for an instant before dimming.

"You know, it's weird," Delores said, twisting open the orange soda. "All the times you think about your dad getting in touch . . . you have these fantasies. You figure he'll ride up one day and say what a mistake he made to ignore you all these years, then take you out and buy you beautiful clothes and a new car or something, and he'll tell you he's really rich and he wants you to come live with him, and he has no other kids, you know, all that stuff. And he'll have some great explanation about why he wasn't in touch, and it will make sense, and you will know, voila, that was the reason all along. Everything clicks into place, and just like that you can go forward."

"But it's not like that," I said. "It's never like that. Whenever I see my dad, it's just this guy who's supposed to be more to me than he is. It's never what you think it will be."

She shook her head.

"No, it isn't," she said.

She started to get gloomy, which can go a long way inside her, so I changed the subject. I started talking about horses. It usually made us feel better. Delores loved Arabs, horses ridden by Bedouins on the Arabian peninsula that are prized for their endurance and elegant posture. I loved paints, the pinto horses bred from crossing quarter horses or Thoroughbreds. We talked about what we liked about each breed, their virtues and shortcomings, and we talked about one day getting two horses and riding them deep into the mountains. Probably in Wyoming, we said, but maybe California. Delores had once run into a fisherman who had taken a horse trip up into the California's Sierra Madres after trout, and for some reason that had stuck with us both.

We talked about riding an Arab and a paint along a trail up a mountain. Maybe, we said, we would spend all summer just drifting and horse camping. We could do that. Cowboys used to do that all the time, which changed the subject a little, because Delores claimed you could still get work as a cowboy. She said they still collected cattle on open range on horseback, and if you were willing to be in a saddle twelve hours a day, and sleep out, you could get work. She wondered what it would be like being a woman doing that kind of work, if the men would leave you alone.

"Here's your pizza," the boy said when he brought it over. "If you want anything like hot peppers or extra cheese, it's up on the condiment table."

"*Merci,*" Delores said, then rattled off something else in her fake French.

"Excuse me?" the boy said, blushing.

Delores whacked some French at him again, and even knowing what she was doing, I couldn't quite tell if she was speaking French. She grinned when she finished, charming as anything, and the boy nodded as if he understood.

"So, you're not from around here?" the boy said.

"We're from Montreal," I said in slow English. "We're French Canadian. My friend doesn't speak much English."

"Ohhhhh," the boy said, as if he had just figured out gravity.

"Can you tell me, please," Delores said in exaggerated English, as she pulled a slice of pizza onto her plate, "whether it's true that Pluto is no longer a planet in the United States?"

"What?" the boy asked.

"Pluto. Is it a planet here?"

The boy cocked his head.

"Oh, you mean, were they from here? In history, you mean?" he asked, which didn't make any sense.

"Are they?" she said, which didn't mean anything either.

The boy mumbled something and excused himself, saying he had to get a pizza out of the oven. Delores watched him go and took a big bite out of her slice. A fleck of tomato sauce touched her cheek and left a shadow there. She grinned.

WE PASSED A COP ON THE WAY OUT OF TOWN. I DROVE. THE pizza box sat between us with four leftover slices for breakfast. The cop car took up a slanted spot, pointed toward us, near an Exxon station at the edge of town. We didn't look left or right. We kept our eyes ahead. I drove two miles per hour below the speed limit. The cop had no reason to stop us unless a taillight had gone out or he happened to be bored.

"Is he coming after us?" Delores whispered.

"No," I said, glancing in the mirror. "I don't think so."

"We're going to have to figure something out," she said.

"What if we changed license plates?"

"That's what I was thinking," Delores said. "That would change our profile."

"You think your dad actually called the police?"

"Hard saying, not knowing," she said, which was a New Hampshire phrase we always used.

I almost missed the turn for the feed store. It looked different at night. When I pulled around the store, I saw another pickup parked near the tent. My lights picked up Julie, who raised her hand to wave. I parked the truck and we slid out.

"Came down to check on you all," Julie said, walking toward us. "Fact is, I was bored at home. Nothing on the TV, and Jack's already asleep. I thought I'd come down and say good night to Speed. I guess I still have that horse bug I can't quite scratch."

"You could have a horse out here," I said. "You've got the land."

"Oh, I suppose," she said. "But Jack said he's tired of the chores and the upkeep. Vet bills, you know. A horse just eats money, but I bet you two know that."

"Still, if you love them," Delores said, "it's worth it."

"I had a friend with a horse, and she let me go over and ride when I liked. That was the best of both worlds. I didn't have to do much for the horse except comb him out when I finished. Beautiful horse, an Arab. Named Lemon."

"Can you still ride him?"

She shook her head.

"The friend died. Breast cancer. And one thing led to another, property sold, and so on. Lemon got bought by a family in Ohio, I think."

"That's too bad," I said.

"You want to ride Speed?" Delores said. "Just bareback for a little?"

Julie didn't say anything. Then she said, "I guess that's what I've been wanting to do."

I grabbed our headlamps out of our truck and handed one to Delores. We kept Julie between us as we walked out toward Speed. The meadow grass had bent over in the first frosts, and now it rested in hummocks and burls. Julie took her time. Once she put her hand on my arm for balance, and afterward I kept my arm out for her to use.

Speed looked up when we reached him, but he had settled into a good round of eating and hardly bothered with us. Julie left the space between us and spent a few minutes petting him. She ran her hands along his back, then down his sides. She combed his mane lightly with her fingers.

"I love every last thing about a horse," she said quietly. "I always have."

"You want to climb up?" Delores asked. "It's no problem."

"Oh, I don't know," she said. "Maybe this is enough."

"We'll give you a hand up," I said. "He won't mind, and he won't go anywhere. He's happy to eat."

"How old is he?" Julie asked, her hands petting him over and over.

"We don't know, really," I said. "He was a pony-ride horse in Massachusetts. The vet who worked on the other horses in the stable took a guess and said over twenty, but he couldn't pin it down much more than that. Might be close to thirty."

"He was probably a handsome boy in his day," she said.

"He's a good horse," I said, and felt my eyes tearing.

"Put me on him," Julie said. "Please."

So we did. Delores stood on one side and I stood on the other and we gave her a hand up. She hung across Speed for a second, and we had to help move her legs around so she could straddle him. Speed lifted his head. She grabbed his mane and sat still for a second.

"He's big," she said. "I guess I didn't realize."

"You want us to walk him a little?" Delores asked.

"No, don't bother. This is plenty. He's done enough for people. It's time he rested."

She leaned over his neck and put her arms around him. She stayed like that. I liked that she didn't care that we were there, or that Speed was just an old, tired horse. She didn't rush, either. She clung to his neck and buried her face in his mane.

"All my horses," she said after a few more minutes, sitting

up, her voice tight, "they're right here in your old buddy Speed. I felt them for just a second."

We didn't say anything. She asked us to help her down. We lowered her carefully off Speed. She dusted her jeans and thanked us. Then we walked her back to her truck.

JULIE LEFT A LITTLE LATER. WE STAYED OUTSIDE AWHILE looking at the stars, but we had trouble staying awake. Around nine we zipped open the tent and climbed into our sleeping bags. It felt good to be inside, to be comfortable and calm, and I knew Delores felt the same way. We didn't talk much. I dug a novel out of my bag—a crazy vampire story, with girls falling in love with bloodsuckers and then turning into flying bats themselves—but I couldn't remember where I had left off. When Delores saw me reading, she asked me to tell her the plot, so I did, and that made us a little edgy because of the vampire theme. Delores wondered why people liked vampires so much, and I told her what someone had told me: that it was the Christ story just reversed, eternal life through blood, and salvation through membership with the host. Delores started laughing.

"So vampires are Jesus?" she asked. "Is that what you're saying? You hatch the craziest ideas, Hattie."

"I'm not saying a vampire *is* Jesus. I'm saying a vampire is appealing because he or she offers eternal life and super-powers. And being a vampire is like being in a club. That's why people like them."

"That's awkward."

"It's a theory," I said, feeling a little annoyed at the way Delores sometimes dismissed what interested me.

"We should write a story about vampire horses," Delores said. "That would be wicked."

I didn't feel like talking, so I read. But Delores decided to be a brat and kept reaching over and pushing my book down. When I didn't respond, she put her hand over the pages so I couldn't read.

"Cut it out," I said.

"Vampire horses could drink people's blood, then pretend they hadn't done a thing. No one would suspect them."

I swatted her hand away.

"Come on," she said. "I'm not sleepy."

I grabbed her hand and bit it.

"Owwww," she said, then spun in her sleeping bag and kicked me with her legs.

I kicked back. We fought like two worms. Delores laughed hard the whole time, but it took me a while to lighten up and get into it. By the time we'd finished, the tent felt warm and close. I shoved her farther to her side. She tried to bite my hands.

"What if a vampire came and stood right outside the tent?" Delores asked. "What would you do then?"

"That's ridiculous."

"Okay, then what's the scariest thing that ever happened to you? No faking."

"You'll get us all crazy and whacked-out with stories."

She spun and kicked me again. I kicked her hard.

"Owwww," she said. "You're a mule."

"I'm tired, Delores."

"Are you fagged?" she asked, using a word we liked to goof with.

"I'm fagged."

"Scariest thing," she said. "Come on."

"You know all my stories," I said. "I have nothing new."

"Okay, I'll tell you mine."

"I know all yours, too."

"No, you don't," she said. "Did I ever tell you about the old drunk on the monkey bars?"

"No," I said. "And I'm not sure I want to hear it."

"You don't know what you're missing."

"Yes, I do," I said. "I'm missing a good night's sleep."

"So, there was this monkey-bar set on the school play-ground where I used to live."

"And you turned into a monkey?"

"No," she said. "One day when the kids got there in the morning, there was a drunk trapped on the monkey bars. He had climbed up or something, and he had fallen through, and he looked all tangled. His leg was up at a weird angle. It was cold, and we had gotten snow, and he wore a dark coat and dark pants. He looked like a crow or something."

"You're making this up."

"So then," she said, her voice going lower, "he started asking us to come over and help him. It was early, and the first teacher was probably on duty, but they used to hang around the door so they could duck in and warm up. And get coffee. All the teachers in that elementary school drank coffee like it was medicine or something."

"So what happened?"

"Nothing. Not for a while. We should have run to get a teacher, but none of us could move. And then Kenny Rider, this complete weirdo, asked if the man had fallen from the sky."

"Get out of here," I said to Delores. "You're crazy."

"He did, too! And I didn't blame him. The guy looked like a warlock who'd been out riding around and suddenly he'd crashed into a jungle gym."

"I thought you said it was monkey bars?"

"Same dif," she said.

"Monkey bars are different from a jungle gym."

"Excuse me, O playground goddess."

"I'm just saying," I said.

"So pretty soon we had about a dozen kids all circled around the *jungle gym*," she said, emphasizing the phrase. "Then the guy looked right at me and said I looked like a sensible sort. He said I should come closer and he would tell me a secret."

"How was this guy caught again?"

"Hattie, quit being such a picky wheezer."

"Well, how can a grown man be held against his will by a jungle gym?"

"He fell from the air, remember, so we figured his arm or leg might be broken. Anyway, he stared at me and asked me to come closer. So I did. I stepped closer and closer. When I was about ten feet away, then nine, then eight, then seven, he nodded and said the thing he had for me was in his hip pocket."

"Get out. What thing?"

"Now, you have to understand this all happened in only three or four minutes. It was weird, I promise. We had the idea that the teachers should be aware of the situation, but that made it more delicious, if you know what I mean. We had something new and different and maybe dangerous right on our playground. I'm telling you, we were all kivvying with excitement."

"And he just happened to single you out?"

"That's right, Hattie brat-face."

"Then what?"

"You don't care. It's just a stupid story."

I squirmed around and kicked her. She kicked me back. We traded kicks until that got boring.

"Speed is a horse vampire," I said.

"So the guy says," Delores said, starting in again, "'Come here, check in my pocket, I got something for you.' And he had this devilish sound to his voice that scared you, but also made you trust him. I don't know. So I went closer to the guy. I can still remember the sound my boots made on that snow. Everything in the world got quiet for a second, and it was just me and that man and my boots squeegeeing. I saw him finally—clearly, I mean. I saw he was just an old drunk. I smelled him, too, like a sewer line, but he looked away as I got near. I guess he knew if he kept looking at me I would run off, but by looking away he made me curious. So I went closer still. I turned around and I made a boy I liked there named Sammy come with me. I motioned him forward and he nodded and took two steps with me. Then he stopped, but I didn't know it."

"And the man turned into a vampire?"

"Almost."

"What then?"

"You need to not be so cynical, that's what, Ms. Hattie brat-head."

"For the love of Pete, what happened?"

"When the guy thought I was close enough, he suddenly turned back to face me. He had taken out one of his eyes somehow, and he'd put his tongue in his cheek, so it looked like he had swallowed his own eye. That's what. He stared at me and our eyes locked, and I thought, Holy crow, he's climbing down the beam of our eyes. You know what I mean. Like we had a laser beam going back and forth, and this nutty man somehow figured out how to shinny along it, and he went right into my head and flew inside there like a bat, and I fell over and started wailing. Then that kid Sammy ran for a teacher, and when they came back, I was still on the ground but the man was gone. The school called the police and made a big ruckus, and the cops tried to talk to me, but it didn't matter what I said. They figured it was some pervy guy preying on kids, and maybe he was, but he was also something more satanic than that. A warlock. That's what it felt like, and he had put a curse on me for a second."

"Are you telling me this really happened, Delores?"

"It did," she said, and I couldn't tell if she was telling tales or meant it.

"What did his voice sound like?" I asked, trying to figure things.

"Like piccolos."

"You mean, all high and everything?"

"Like birds."

We didn't say anything after that. Later on I found her curled next to me, spooning, her face scrunched and troubled with something in her dreams. I thought about waking her up but decided against it. Then I thought about Speed, and the Fergusons, and what we were really doing out here in Wisconsin. The whole thing didn't make much sense when you faced it down, but in my gut I felt like it meant something good and important. Maybe we both needed this trip to cut away from something behind us. I thought about Delores's dad and his threat to call the cops, and I figured he probably had done that, had probably seized the moment to bully his ex-wife. Sometimes people needed to be right no matter who it hurt or how useless it was to take a stand. All that thinking made it hard to sleep, so I poked my head out and saw Speed eating grass near our tent. I listened to him yanking up mouthfuls and slobbering it down, and when he passed by I saw his silhouette blacked out against the white of the meadow and he looked as pretty as a horse could look, and as proud.

JULIE GAVE US TWO AGRICULTURAL LICENSE PLATES OFF some old farm equipment stored behind the barn. Delores had told her the situation, and Julie hadn't batted an eye.

"I have no idea if these will do you any good," she said, supervising us as we took off the plates with an old, rusty screwdriver. "In fact, they may land you in more trouble if they're out of date, but you're welcome to them. You stick to the back roads and you may do okay. You look like farm girls running errands. Once you get out of Wisconsin, the cops won't know as much about the plates."

"Women going west," Delores said, chipping rust off the screws that held the plates to the old baler.

"It's a grand adventure," Julie said, "and you aren't hurting anyone. But mark this address down, though, and if you get in any trouble and need to dump old Speed, we can keep him here for a while."

"Thank you," I said.

I stood drinking coffee. Julie had brought us coffee

and muffins from town. I had a blueberry nut muffin and a warm cup of coffee. The temperature had dropped, and the meadow looked white and furled. Speed kept his nose buried in the grass. Julie had already been out to him with carrots. That's when Delores explained our pickle.

Delores popped the first license plate and handed it to me. She went to work on the second.

"Do me one favor, though, will you, girls?" Julie asked. "You call home now and then so people don't worry too much. You'd be surprised how much parents miss you and think about you when you're gone."

"Not my mom," Delores said, concentrating on the plate.

"Even your mom," Julie said, sipping her own coffee. "Even if she doesn't seem like she would. I don't know her, but I know moms. She'll worry, trust me."

We didn't say anything for a while after that. It felt good to be outside early. We turned now and then to watch Speed drift by. Then Julie told us she always thought South Dakota was a good place for horses, and that it was closer than Wyoming or Montana. She talked about prairie grass, which had once spread all over the Midwest and behaved like a sea, actually. A sea of grass going on forever. She said the bison ate the grass, then spread it as manure, and they trampled the ground and aerated it for centuries. The topsoil in the grasslands once held the thickness of a chocolate layer cake, dense and sweet, and she thought a horse could get by there nicely.

"I wish I had a friend in South Dakota," she said as Delores got the second plate free. "Someone to send you to, you know. I'd feel better if you had a destination."

"We've got a list of rangelands," I said.

Julie nodded.

I put the plates on our vehicles while Delores and Julie struck the tent and collected our sleeping bags. At one point Jack came out and asked if she intended to open the store, and Julie shushed him away, saying if he wanted the store open he could do it himself. He didn't seem to like that answer, and went off shaking his head. Julie stuck out her tongue at him. We all laughed.

She asked if she could bring Speed into the trailer, and we said of course.

You could tell by the way she handled him that she loved horses. Speed was just one more horse, true, but with her hands and her voice, she talked to every horse she had ever known. She stopped him a couple times to lean into him and put her cheek against his flesh. She hugged him before she sent him into the trailer. He went without a protest.

"That's a nice horse," she said, her eyes full. "He's a gentle thing."

"We want to thank you for everything you've done for us," I said. "It really helped us out."

"It helped me out, too. You do me a favor and call home. And if you get a chance, I'd love to get a card knowing how you two fared. It's like a story, and I want to hear to the end, 'cause it's going to drive me crazy wondering about it."

"We'll send a note," Delores said. "I'll make Hattie write it. She's the bookish one."

Julie hugged us both.

"You two stick together," she said. "Don't let a stupid boy get between you. You're good friends. You stay that way."

We nodded. I climbed in behind the wheel and started up the truck. It knocked a little but then found its idle. Julie stepped back, and we rocked slowly over the grass and hummocks. Before we turned onto the highway, we turned and waved. Julie watched us go. She raised her hand but she didn't wave.

DELORES DID HER TOENAILS MOST OF THE MORNING. SHE could take longer to do her nails than anyone I had ever known. She put on the radio, and we sang along when we knew the words. Delores said Ruby Red Party, her nail polish, smelled like old ladies. She waited until the road got straight and flat to do the edges. She hated messing up the sides. When she finished, she screwed the top back onto the bottle and moved her feet around on the dash until the sun hit her toes.

"There," she said. "I am more beautiful than ever."

"You're nuts," I said.

"I'm going to turn on the phone," she said. "Check to see if we have any bars. And maybe I can retrieve some messages."

"Okay."

"Where are we, anyway?"

"We're in Minnesota. We have been for a while."

"What do we have? Two more days, maybe?"

I shrugged. Taking the back roads meant a longer trip.

"Here goes," she said, flipping open her phone and putting it to her ear.

"Messages," she whispered.

She listened for a while. At one point she leaned forward and turned off the radio. She flicked at something on her foot, keeping it away from her toes. She nodded. Then she touched my arm and nodded again.

"That's awkward," she said, flipping the phone closed.

"What is?"

"One message was from Paulette, going mental. Her

sister Regina is pregnant and her whole family is going nuts. She wants to come out and join us. She said she could fly and meet us somewhere."

"That's not happening," I said.

Delores shook her head.

"Your mom called, too," she said. "Just the usual stuff. She's worried and wanted an update."

"What else?"

"My dad notified the police. It's turned into a big freaking showdown between my mom and him. I'm eighteen, though, so it's not clear what they can do to us. You're sixteen. That's the problem. And my cousin Richard is being a dink about the horse trailer. Suddenly he needs it. He called and said he didn't want to press charges, but he was thinking about it. What a bunch of ridiculous people."

"Maybe we should just get to South Dakota," I said.

"I have pretty toes," Delores said, pointing to her feet. "No one can stop me."

"Do you think your dad really notified the police, or is it just a trick to get us to turn around?"

"Hard saying, not knowing," Delores said. "But here's what I don't get. No one cares when we're around, but the minute we leave, we're everyone's top priority. It's weird."

"You want the thing you don't have."

"That's for certain. I mean," she said, shifting again to set her toes in the sun, "it's not like we stole anything of value. Speed was heading to the glue factory. The stupid trailer was sitting behind Richard's house with grass growing up through the floor. It's all about power. Who can bully who."

"They don't like seeing us free," I said, understanding something for the first time.

"That's right. If one person wears a ball and chain, they want everyone to wear one. You know what I should do? I should call my dad and say, 'Gee, you're right, could you send me a couple thousand dollars and I'll jump on a plane and come live with you?' Then we'd see how important it all is to him."

"They wouldn't care if we were boys. If we were boys, they'd say we were boys being boys. But girls are supposed to be home sitting around. I hate that."

"The history of Western society is one long attempt to control the sexual and reproductive autonomy of women," Delores said. She looked at me and puffed out her cheeks and crossed her eyes. We both laughed hard.

"Where in the world did you come up with that one?" I asked her.

"It's the only thing I remember from school. The *only thing*! Ms. Blankley. You remember. She was right out of college and she spouted all this feminist junk, and everyone hated her. I did, too. But when you kind of stopped and listened, you realized she made sense about eighty percent of the time. And she said that. In fact, it was on the top of most of her handouts. We used to have these crazy arguments in her class about men and women and gender roles. You know, women as property, the whole white dress thing at weddings. We had about three fundamentalist Christians in the class, and they went cowabunga every time she got wound up. The school let her go that spring."

"What class?"

"This kind of lit/sociology class called The Outsiders. Who was outside of whom. You know, groups within groups. It was interesting, sort of. We read a couple good books."

The phone rang.

"I forgot to turn it off," Delores said. "Should we answer?"

"Who is it?"

She looked at the phone cover.

"I don't recognize the number. It might be my dad."

"Your call," I said. "No pun intended."

"I haven't talked to him in forever. And now he probably wants to yell at me."

She reached forward and lowered the volume on the radio.

"Hello?" she asked, flicking open her phone.

Someone said something.

"Oh, hello, Dad," she said, making her eyes big for my benefit. "How have you been?"

She listened.

"Well," she said after a little while, "that's one way to see it. I don't think that's the only way. Mom has been fine."

She listened some more.

Then, without saying anything else, she closed the phone. It rang again almost immediately.

"That was bad Daddy," she said. "The angry idiot Daddy who doesn't listen."

"You hung up on him?"

"You can't hang up a cell phone."

"You know what I mean," I said.

She opened the phone again.

"Listen," she said when he apparently paused. "If you just want to call and yell, I'm going to hang up. . . . Yes. That's right. I expect to discuss things rationally. You speak, then I speak. We come to a middle ground or something. I'm eighteen, as you just pointed out. I don't want to be . . ."

She turned to me and raised her eyebrows in question.

"Berated?" I whispered.

"Berated," she said into the phone.

Then she listened. He went on for a long time, but at least he didn't seem to be yelling.

"I don't see how calling the police will help anyone," she said after a few minutes. "It's not going to improve the situation to have us arrested somewhere. If you think that will teach us a big lesson or something, I guess you can do it. But I'm here to tell you that it won't be a lesson. It will just make things more difficult for everyone. And if Richard needs the trailer, you can tell him to rent one and I will reimburse him for any costs. I've got waitressing money left over."

I heard his voice come loudly and abruptly over the phone.

"Then what is the point? Is it that this trailer is so incredibly valuable? He can take a horse from here to there in a rented trailer. It will probably be a nicer trailer if he rents one. You're grabbing at something to make it into an issue, and it really isn't an issue. You're just trying to find some kind of leverage."

Then he yelled again. She snapped the phone closed.

"You were amazing," I said.

"If you stay real calm with people, you can usually poke holes through whatever they're doing to you."

"Still," I said.

"He's just threatening. I don't know, maybe he'll go

ahead and do it, but he hasn't yet. Alerted the police, I mean. But it's going to sound pretty flimsy. He's being a big freaking buzz kill."

"Is your mom freaking?"

"Just because he's involved," Delores said. "She digs the attention. Are you kidding? Mom is an attention sponge, especially from men."

"Father issues," I said, and we both laughed.

"The long and the short of it is," Delores said, "they can't stand not having us under their power. They can't stand that we're doing something spur-of-the-moment. They don't say a word about Speed anymore. They stopped playing that card."

"Speed's the whole reason for the trip."

"Speed's part of the reason," Delores said. "We've got to be honest about that. There's other stuff, and we both know it."

"True. I'll give you that."

"Just stuff. Just yearning."

"We're in Minnesota," I said. "That's got to count for something."

Chapter 5

"WAKE UP," DELORES SAID, SHAKING MY KNEE. "YOU HAVE to see this."

I woke slowly. Rain hit against the windshield. I couldn't tell how long I had been asleep. It felt like late afternoon. We had stopped too much and made herky-jerky time. I rubbed my face and tilted the rearview mirror to see my reflection. I looked swollen and squinty at the same time. "Ugh," I said, and dug out a brush from the space between the seat cushions. I ran the brush through my hair until I didn't have nap head. Then I drank a big gulp of cherry water. When I finished, I put my head back against the seat and tried to wake up. But my brain buzzed, and the windshield wipers hypnotized me.

"We're taking a little break," Delores said. "We're going to have a cultural experience."

"Oh?" I said, not really getting into it.

She veered off the highway. She tilted the rearview mirror back to where she could use it.

"We've got to get Speed out for a while, anyway. And we have to see this."

"See what?"

"You'll see. Kiss my hand in gratitude," she said, holding out her right hand like a princess.

"You're nuts."

"You will when you see what I've found. You will."

"I'm hungry," I said.

"Oh, I'll take care of that, too," she said.

"You've done all this while I was sleeping?"

"You moaned in your sleep. I think you were having a sex dream."

"You're insane."

"What, you never have sex dreams?"

"Oh, Lord, don't start on your sex chats."

"Hold on," she said. "I have to see where I'm going."

I saw the sign when she did.

SPAM MUSEUM

"You're kidding me," I said.

"Did I say you would want to kiss my hand?" she asked, holding it out again.

"*The* SPAM factory?"

"It's got to be."

I sat up.

"Let's go," I said.

"I'm going."

"What time is it? Will it be open?"

"It's like four-fifteen. I figure it's open until five at least."

We followed the signs. The parking lot was nearly empty. Delores parked as close to the door as she could. I jumped out, checked on Speed, told him we weren't delivering him to the SPAM factory, then grabbed Delores's hand and sprinted with her to the entrance.

A slender young black guy in a red jacket took our money. He told us we only had thirty minutes, but if we wanted to buy anything from the shop, they would let us browse awhile longer. We thanked him and ran through the enormous SPAM can that served as the front door. The lobby had a wall of SPAM cans stacked to the ceiling. Delores took out her cell phone and made me stand in front of it while she took three pictures. Then I took three of her. The ticket guy saw we wanted a picture together and came out from behind his booth window and snapped two for us.

"That's a SPAM dandy shot," Delores said, looking at the picture when he handed back the phone.

"You better move it along," he said, heading back to his booth.

"SPAM you very much," Delores said.

I grabbed her hand and yanked her into the museum. We had trouble slowing down. Each new display was more delicious. We stayed awhile in front of an exhibit on the history of Hormel meats. We read about Slammin' Spammy, a bomb-throwing pig from World War II, and Hormel Dog Dessert in a tube, and Wimpy's eight-ounce hamburger in a can. We watched a clip of the Hormel Girls, a group of young women who traveled the country singing and dancing and promoting SPAM, and read a few pages of *Squeal,* the Hormel meatpacking magazine. Delores sighed and said she wished she could be a Hormel Girl, dancing around the country in a crazy outfit. Then we moved faster, because the single docent—a large, bright red woman who cleared her throat a couple times and began moving a chair to where it apparently spent the night—seemed to be readying to close. We read a quick article about a SPAM-carving contest in

Seattle and watched a three-minute Monty Python skit about SPAM in Britain.

"I want a T-shirt," Delores said.

"It's not in our budget."

"To heck with the budget. This is the SPAM Museum, for goodness' sakes, Hattie."

We shopped. The shop had coffee cups, postcards, stationery, calendars, alarm clocks, and wastebaskets—everything SPAM themed. We spent a long time searching through the T-shirts. Delores debated between a pale yellow shirt that said *SPAM-Fabulous* over a faded picture of a SPAM can, and a second shirt that said *SPAM Saved the Russian Army, Nikita Khrushchev*. The Russian army marched clockwise around the shirt.

I bought a straight navy T-shirt with a bright yellow can of SPAM across the chest.

"Which?" Delores said, pointing to the shirts.

"I like the Russian army one," I said.

"I do, too, but I like the other one better."

"What does that mean?"

"The Russian shirt feels like it's trying too hard," Delores said. "I can just picture guys reading the shirt and staring at my boobs. 'SPAM-Fabulous' is easy."

"Okay," I said. "Buy it."

She bought both. She couldn't help it. She wanted to buy us hats, too, but I told her no way. She pitched a mini-fit, but she couldn't help laughing as she paid. When the clock in the shop hit five, it let out five oinks.

"You all find everything?" the ticket guy asked.

"You bet your SPAM we did," Delores said, crazy, the way she can be at times.

"Is that your truck?" he asked. "Because there was a cop looking at it a second ago."

"We're fugitives from the law," Delores said. "We're women going west."

"Exciting," the ticket guy said.

"Where's the cop now?" I asked.

"He went over near the other side of the parking lot. Be cool going out, not all spazzy. That's my advice."

"SPAM you again," Delores said.

The ticket guy shook his head and smiled down at his hands.

The rain hadn't let up. We stood for a minute under the archway of the SPAM can.

"Where are we, anyway?" I asked.

"Austin, Minnesota. We haven't come that far across Minnesota yet."

"What's the next state?" I asked, crooking my head

forward a little to look out for the cop car. I saw it down where the SPAM guy had said it would be. It idled quietly, its lights dimmed, the cop impossible to see through the window.

"South Dakota," Delores said.

"We should change the plates back," I said.

"I'm thinking so, too."

"Let's find a place where Speed can feed and we can get out of the rain. We can figure the rest out later."

"Where, though?"

"No idea," I said. "Let's just follow the service road and see where it takes us. It's not like it's all city around here."

"That's a plan."

We put the T-shirt bags over our heads and ran back to the truck. We knew better than to look at the cop car. Delores jumped in behind the wheel, and I slid in on the other side. She started the truck and got it going smoothly. She drove pretty smart, actually. She looped a little toward the cop car, no worries, then steered her way out of the parking lot.

"Is he coming?" she asked, not looking in the mirror. "Pretend you need something behind you and turn and look."

I did.

"Nope, he's not coming."

"We are so freaking ninja."

She gassed the truck onto the service road. We headed west.

"I get to wear your T-shirt half the time," I said.

"Which one?"

"Whichever one I want."

"We're not sleeping out tonight," she said, looking at the rain.

"We can get a motel," I said. "That's in the budget, but not the T-shirts."

"Two nights in a motel," she said. "Right?"

"Whatever," I said. "We'll see."

"We need a sweet setup with Speed."

"He needs to take a break soon."

I got up on my knees and looked back through the rear window at Speed. Now and then I glimpsed him swaying between his two halter leads. His big, lanky head swung into view for a second. He looked asleep.

"I hate putting him out in the rain," I said. "Even with a blanket, I don't like it."

"He'll be okay. We've had good luck so far. Besides, if he's going to be living in the wild, he better get used to a few things."

For a while after that we didn't talk. I'm not sure what Delores thought about, but I felt a little homesick and lonely.

I couldn't say why. Part of it came from the isolation of being in a truck, on a road, in a state we didn't know. Part of it came from wondering if we were doing right by Speed after all. Maybe it had been selfish to take him, just as the Fergusons had said. We sort of used him as an excuse to leave, it felt like, and that put a block of ice in my guts. But then I reminded myself that I loved Speed, truly loved him, and what came from love had a chance of being right. I wouldn't hurt him for the world.

We passed two motels, one skeezier than the next. Each tried to outdo the other with catchy names. Bide-a-While, and Empty Tank Motel. You had to wonder about the owners, the first time they opened for business, the whole crew standing out in the front yard of the cruddy-looking place and seeing that sign and thinking, *That will really bring them in.* The image seemed so crazy, I had to rub my hands into my eyes.

"Let's get Speed out," I said. "He's been cooped up too long."

"Okay, Hattie," Delores said, taking a turn up one of the side roads. "There's bound to be a meadow around here."

A mile or two up, Delores bounced the truck up a dirt road that went through two meadows. The land stretched out flat and quiet and dark. The rain had stopped for the most part, but the clouds had covered any chance of a moon, and Delores turned on her lights to see ahead of us.

"Look at that," I said. "Did you see?"

Just over the next small rise we saw a pack of horses. They had collected next to the road under a large pin oak. In the gloaming light, with the clouds low over the horizon, the horses looked out of a painting.

"Pull over," I said, but Delores was already doing it.

"There's a gate, too," Delores said. "Sweet. Spammy sweet."

She pulled carefully onto the shoulder, which was wide enough to get us entirely off the road. The meadows went on in either direction as far as we could see. Here and there the landowner had left a tree, but mostly the land threw up grass.

I hopped out as soon as the truck switched off and opened the trailer. Speed stepped a few times in place, nervous at the smell of other horses. I made a quiet humming sound, as I usually did around horses, and I edged in and unbuckled his halter leads. Delores opened the pasture gate as I backed him down. He had crapped a couple times and the trailer floor was messy.

"You've got some friends," I said to Speed, turning him to the pasture gate.

"You don't think they'll challenge him, do you?" Delores asked. "The males, I mean."

"No, I don't think so. He's too old. No one will take him as a threat."

"Let's hope not."

She swung the gate back. I let Speed go through. He walked ahead, stiff from all the confinement. A horse in the pack whinnied, but I couldn't tell which one. Delores closed the gate, and we put our elbows on it.

"'He is pure air and fire; and the dull elements of earth and water never appear in him, but only in patient stillness while his rider mounts him: he is indeed a horse; and all other jades you may call beasts,'" I quoted, watching Speed pick his way into the meadow.

"Oh, geez, Hattie, don't start with all that."

"It's the only horse quote I know."

"Where's it from again?"

"Shakespeare. I forget which play. I learned it in fifth grade. I used to look up horse quotes. I thought it made horses sound cool."

"And made you sound like a dork."

"I'm starving."

We didn't move away, though. We watched Speed bury his nose in the grass. Mist drifted over him in pale puffs, and sometimes he disappeared in the dimness, and other times he reappeared, a dark horse shape moving gently over the flat ground.

WHILE I CHANGED THE LICENSE PLATES BACK TO NEW Hampshire tags, Delores dug around in the truck and came up with peanut butter sandwiches. Just peanut butter on the heels of our last loaf of bread. She mixed up cherry water and found half a bag of Cool Ranch Doritos. We ate on the tailgate of the truck. The weather began to clear, but it was still misty and cool, and we both wore barn coats and baseball hats. Enough moonlight fell through the clouds so that we didn't need headlamps.

"You ever wonder," I asked her, chomping down on three Doritos at once, "how we got here? I mean, do you think we were destined to end up in Austin, Minnesota, or wherever we are, or that this was all by our choice and it's just a random set of circumstances?"

"If this is fate, it sucks," Delores said.

"What, you don't like being here?"

Delores looked around.

"Actually, I do," she said. "As long as some hillbilly Bob

doesn't come along and drag us out of the truck tonight. It's pretty here."

"I don't think anyone's around," I said. "Besides, we've got a can of pepper spray."

"I think," Delores said, stuffing the last of her sandwich into her mouth and talking around it, "that maybe we're living in Speed's fate. Like maybe he's pulling us along. Who knows? And maybe we were Roman gladiators ten lives ago and Speed was the Emperor Augustus or something."

"You are weird," I said.

"I'm going to check on Speed. You finish the excellent meal I made you. Why didn't we buy SPAM for sandwiches?"

She grabbed her headlamp and pushed through the gate. As soon as it clicked, she seemed to disappear. I ate the rest of my sandwich and all of the remaining Doritos, but it felt strange sitting alone in the darkness. I stood and brushed the crumbs off my lap. I started to call Delores's name, but that seemed wimpy. I crumpled up the Doritos bag and stuffed it into the old bread sack. I wiped my mouth and had a last drink of cherry water. A chill made me shudder a little, and I grabbed my headlamp and headed for the gate. Before I reached it, I saw Delores riding up on the other side of the fence. She rode a horse, but it wasn't Speed.

"Thoroughbreds, Hattie," she whispered loudly. "This one let me right up on her."

"Are you kidding me?"

"Come on. We could ride any one we like. I think they're racehorses."

I pushed through the gate. Delores sat astride a beautiful bay mare with a white blaze on its forehead. Being around Speed so much, I had nearly forgotten what a horse could be. Delores had her hands dug into the horse's mane. She looked wild and happy.

"Speed's fine," she said. "I saw him out by the other horses. Come on. Jump up on one, and we'll ride like Sioux warriors."

I felt my heart go up as it always did when I was about to ride. I jogged beside Delores as she trotted the horse back to the pack. It was hard to make out the horses' individual shapes until I was nearly up to them. But I saw the one I wanted almost at once. It was a big white male, thicker than the others through the withers, with a soft, gentle face. I stepped between a couple horses and moved closer. He let me pet him without a problem. Delores kept her horse on the outside of the small herd.

"You taking that white one?" she said in a stage whisper.

"I hope so."

"Hop up. Can you get on him?"

"I'm trying," I said.

"Giddyup, girl. Come on."

I pushed my body close, grabbed a hank of his mane, and jumped. He shied a step or two back, but I had a hold on him and let him carry me for a second. When he steadied, I dropped again, bounced, and chucked my body up over his back. He put his head down to keep eating. I swung my leg around and grabbed his mane on either side of his neck.

"Come on, boy," I said, and got his head up out of the grass.

Then I kicked him a little and goosed him forward. He went without any difficulty. I kicked him again, and he moved better, nearly trotting until I pulled him up beside Delores's bay. It felt amazing to have a horse under me and the night clearing off.

"Now, this is more like it," Delores said.

"I'll follow," I said.

"Easy does it," she said, and pulled her bay toward the center of the meadow.

She walked at first. I had a little trouble figuring out how to go bareback, although it wasn't the first time I'd ridden that way. But the white horse was new to me, and I didn't want to spook him or let him get away with being stupid. I stayed firm on him, riding him with my hips and legs, while his head stroked up and down between my hands. "Good boy, good boy," I whispered. I concentrated so hard on getting my rhythm with him that I didn't notice the moonlight at first. It came out low and haunted, stretched across the hillside, and I saw Delores kick her horse into a trot. My horse surged right after the bay, and we caught up to her in no time. We cantered a little, and the moon blazed on Delores uphill from me, and my heart filled. I started tearing, not sure why, but horses did that to me and I didn't question it. It had something to do with the moonlight, the mist rising off the meadow, the clouds pushing east along the horizon. But it also had something to do with Delores and me, about a yearning we both had, a feeling that time might run out on us somehow and we wouldn't know it had until it was too late.

Then we galloped.

"All other jades you may call beasts," I whispered, and leaned down to stay close to the white horse's neck.

The horses felt full of the whole thing, too. I knew it. They ran straight ahead, ears back, their long pulling gaits pegged to a Thoroughbred's stride. They threw their hind legs through their front legs, their big haunches yanking and shoving, their mouths and necks starting to sweat. I gripped harder. Up ahead of me Delores let out a war whoop, and then we crested a hill I hadn't even noticed, and headed down. I smelled a river somewhere, or at least water, and the drops from my horse came up in white dots around me, the hooves casting spray from the wet grass, and when I checked Delores, she appeared to be running on a lake top, a girl on a fairy horse sprinting across fresh water. As I looked, Delores let go of the bay's mane and sat straight up, riding only with her legs and hips, her arms out as if to fly. She tilted her head back, too, and she looked so perfect doing it that I didn't dare try to copy her. This was something only for her, something I could only witness, and she galloped down that hill with her soul somewhere up in the sky above her. We both knew it, and we never had to mention it.

THE HORSES STOPPED NEAR A TREE LINE WHERE I GUESSED a river or stream ran. A few stars came out ahead of us, and by seeing them I knew the weather had broken for the time being. Still, the air hit cold and clean along my chest, but down under my seat, and along my legs—any place I touched against the white horse—warmth passed to me. The horses breathed hard. Delores had returned her hands to the horse's mane, and she breathed as deeply as the horse did. I laughed, but it wasn't a loud, funny laugh. It felt almost like a cough.

"You okay?" I asked.

"Yes," she said.

"I've never ridden a finer horse."

"Faster, anyway. Speed's still the finest horse."

"You're a beautiful rider, Delores," I said.

"You, too."

"We are Sioux," I said.

"We are Sioux," she answered.

Then we did something we hadn't done in a long while. We lay backward along the horses' spines, our heels up on either side of the horses' necks. It's a tricky thing to do, a move that can easily backfire, but we'd done it a lot the previous summer for a string of days. We'd taken Speed to the Chalk Stream every day, and one of the other horses, too, and we'd lounged on the horses' backs, watching the blue summer sky pass, the shade running like dark cats across our skin. That's what we did for a while in the field outside of Austin, Minnesota. We didn't speak for a long time. It was enough to have horses under us, their hay smell and sweat mixing in the September winds, and the sound, now and then, of water running over stones.

"Stars are coming out," Delores said when we had cooled and the horses had started to nose the grass.

"I love horses," I said.

"I know you do, Hattie."

"You know I love Speed, don't you?"

"Sure," she said.

"I want him to have some sort of great day," I said. "That sounds stupid, I know."

"No, it doesn't," she said, then changed the subject a little. "Are the stars spinning above you?"

"Yes. Like a big tube and the horse is at the bottom."

"I don't care what happens. They can arrest me, and I'm still glad we came. I am. I bet Speed feels that way, too."

"I feel a little lost, though," I said.

"Whoa!" Delores said. "I almost fell. We're all lost, Hattie, one way or another. This old guy I met once said the trick of life is to stop thinking it's about sitting on a train until the next stop."

"What is it, then?"

"Who knows? But if you keep expecting the next station to appear and all lights to be on, you're probably going to be disappointed. I think that was his point. You might ride for days on the train and not see anything. And other times you'd make three stops in an hour. He said the trick is to learn to ride the train."

"He sounds like a dope," I said, and started to laugh.

Delores laughed, too.

"I'm cold," she said. "Let's go."

We walked the horses back up the hill and slid off them when we came close to the herd. We spent a few minutes with Speed. He looked old and tired beside the younger horses, but he didn't want for anything. He had plenty of grass and some good company. It occurred to me, and maybe to Delores, too, that we could drive away and leave him right where he stood. It was possible no one would notice him for a week or more, and when they did, he would be their horse. He could stay with the small herd, or maybe someone would bring him into a warm barn for the winter. But maybe what we wanted for him was something without fences.

We didn't talk about it. We went back to the truck and climbed in and ran the engine for a few minutes to take the chill off. Then we fluffed out the sleeping bags and lay down feet to head on the bench seat. I told Delores her feet smelled like coffee cans, and she pushed them into my face a little, but it wasn't that kind of mood. Frost came in and covered the windshield, and before she fell asleep, Delores made sure we had the pepper spray ready. I put it on the dashboard near me. We didn't tell any scary stories that night, and we didn't talk for more than a minute. Cold wrapped around the truck, and sometime during the night I heard sleet tick off the cab roof and the hiss of wind throwing it against the trees.

Chapter 6

WE WOKE TO WHITE FIELDS.

"I'm freezing," Delores said first thing when she felt me moving.

I couldn't see her. She had the sleeping bag over her head.

"Start the engine a little," I said. "I'm going to check on Speed. It snowed."

"Did not," she said, sitting up and looking around. She looked sleepy and confused.

"Holy moley," she said, sliding back under the sleeping bags. "Let's keep sleeping."

"Get the truck running. I'm starving for real."

She didn't budge. I punched her hip a little with my hand,

but she didn't move. So I made an annoying squeaking sound I knew she hated, until she finally shoved up and jumbled the sleeping bags toward me.

"You are such a brat," she said.

"I'm cold and I'm hungry," I said. "Now get moving."

I pushed out of the truck and nearly fell. Ice coated the road. I heard the truck clatter a little, then turn on. The horses looked up, their ears twitching to check us out. I opened the gate and stepped through.

I saw him right away.

A stone rolled through my guts, and I opened my mouth to try for air.

"No, no, no," I said, and I ran.

The closest horses to the gate spread at my approach, spooked by my sliding, spastic run. I fell once onto a knee and shot back up. I yelled for Delores but doubted she heard me. I yelled again anyway, because Speed lay on the ground, his body a black line in a white field, the snow and sleet covering him.

"No, no," I said, and slid down on my knees next to his head.

I knew better than to put my arms around his neck so suddenly, and he jerked up, frightened, his cheek slamming into my nose. A bright light cracked in my skull, and Speed waved his hooves against the ground. I fell backward, stupefied, and the pain of his thick head hitting me climbed down into my neck, then my shoulders, and would have kept going if a bright red stream of blood hadn't suddenly spouted onto my coat.

"Easy," I said, but whether I was talking to him or myself, I couldn't say.

I sawed the back of my hand across my face, and it came away bloody. I arched my head out like a chicken pecking, trying to keep the blood off my coat, at the same time trying to see what had happened to Speed. He looked horrible, glazed with ice and suffering. Steam came off his body. I reached out my hand and put it on his head. Ice shucked under my fingers when I ran my hand down his neck. He had moved just enough at my hug to show me a snow horse, a shadow of his shape blocking out the snow.

I ran back to the truck.

"Delores!" I yelled, and she finally came out, stepping out of the driver's side and looking over the roof at me. I watched her take in the blood, her face puzzled. Then she leaned a little to her left and saw past me to Speed.

"Are you kidding me?" she said, her voice rising.

"He's down," I said.

"Did he get you with a hoof?"

"No, he lifted his head into mine. He's alive."

"Let me get something. Hold on."

She brought out a paper bag and hurried around the truck. She crumpled it and handed it to me.

"Just hold this against your nose for a second," she said. "I don't have anything else right now. You're bleeding like a stuck pig."

"Fill a plastic bag with snow," I said, my voice high and tight and nasal.

She nodded. She zipped back around the truck and dug inside until she came up with an olive plastic grocery bag. She held it open and brushed snow and sleet off the hood and roof. I stood still and pressed the paper bag against my nose, trying not to notice if the blood came faster or slower. I glanced down once and saw bloodstains all over the front of my jacket and down on my jeans.

"Here you go," she said, coming around.

I started to reach for the bag, but then a wing beat of nausea hit me and I held up a finger to her. I stepped a couple paces away and vomited. It killed my nose to vomit. Delores came over and held my hair back. I vomited twice before I could straighten up. My ribs scraped against something that must have been skin or muscle.

"Are you okay?" Delores said, giving me the bag.

I nodded. The ice didn't feel like anything on my nose.

"We've got to get your head tilted back," she said. "You're still gushing."

"It'll be all right," I said, tasting ropes of blood spooling down my throat.

"Maybe, maybe not," she said, trying to see past my hand and the bag of ice. "We may have to have you looked at."

"It's just a bloody nose," I said. "What about Speed?"

"Let me take a look," she said. "You get in the truck and warm up."

"I'm coming with you," I said.

She didn't try to argue. I held the bag against my nose and walked with her over to the gate. The horses didn't scatter this time. They milled away, curious and interested, their profiles to us sometimes as if ready to run. Delores made a little "shoo, shoo, shoo" sound that kept them pushing away. Ice still tried to trip me up, and once I had to stop and let my feet slide me a little downhill. The pin oak near the gate looked glassy and cold.

"Okay," Delores said to Speed from a distance, talking to him the way I should have done. She wanted him to know we were approaching. "Okay, Speedy boy."

"He looks bad," I said.

"Just hold on," she said. "Let's stay calm."

She knelt down softly next to him. I followed her. He turned his head a bit to look at us, his brown eye rolling to focus. He appeared nervous and scared.

"Do you think he got cold or something?" I asked. "You think that's it?"

She shrugged. She kept petting him. Ice followed the blade of her hand.

"It could be anything," she said after a little while. "He could have slipped, or his gut got twisted. Who knows? He's old, Hattie."

"He can't do this," I said. "Not this."

My eyes filled. It felt like a big train, one you figured would arrive any second but seemed to delay and delay and delay, suddenly snapped across a trestle above your head and sucked all the wind from everywhere so that no one could breathe. I looked at Speed, then had to turn away.

"Is your nose slowing down?" Delores asked, not looking at me.

I pulled the plastic bag away. I put the back of my fingers under my nostrils. Only a little blood leaked out on them.

"I'm fine," I said, daubing the fingers on my jeans.

"We could try to get him onto his feet. Maybe with both of us he might be talked into it."

"It's worth a try."

Delores grabbed his halter and I walked around his head, near where his hooves were, and grabbed the other side.

"Ready?" she said.

I nodded and put down the bag of ice. A second later she raised her voice and said, "Come on, Speed. Up you go. Come on. Get up," and I did the same from my side. We both tugged at the halter straps but he wasn't having any. His head thumped down after he raised it a little. He nickered and something sounded deep and raspy in his chest.

I got up and walked away. I put my hands on my knees and I felt like vomiting again. Only now it wasn't my nose that turned my stomach, but Speed's flaccid body. I took deep, even breaths, trying to sort things out.

"We need a vet," I said straight out, not turning to make sure Delores heard.

She didn't say anything.

"They must have one around here," I said, then turned back to see her.

"The thing is, Hattie," Delores said slowly. "We probably need a gun."

▸ ▸ ▸ ▸

We sat in the truck, our feet up to the heat coming in from below. We had the blower on at its highest level. I liked the sound of it. It blocked out everything for a second or two so I didn't have to think. My nose felt flat and spread-out against my face. I still tasted blood now and then, and dry kernels flaked away sometimes from somewhere inside my head, and it felt like paint coming off a wall. My jacket front had turned rusty and brown. Blood had dotted my jeans with dull pennies of color.

I didn't look at Speed. I couldn't.

"The Fergusons were right all along," I said after a little while.

"You don't know that yet," Delores said. "Don't jump to conclusions."

"You just said we needed a gun. You know how things stand as well as I do."

She didn't say anything to that.

"I'm just trying to think," Delores said after a bit. "We need to eat soon no matter what. I'm going to chew my fingers if we don't get something."

"I can't eat," I said.

"We're eating," she said. "What day is it?"

"Saturday, I think."

"I'm eighteen, so someone will sell me a gun. I don't know if they sell them on Saturdays, though."

"That's crazy."

She shrugged. She moved her feet to get them in the line of the air blower.

"I did this to him," I said, my eyes getting cloudy again. "To Speed. I should have let him go."

"Nobody did anything to anybody. He's just old, Hattie. It's not like we didn't know something like this could happen."

I forced myself to look out at the meadow. Speed still lay where we had left him. The other horses had wandered off a couple hundred yards. I couldn't stand seeing him all by himself in the snow.

"Why don't you go and get some food?" I said. "Bring some back. And if you can get a gun, go ahead. Use the money."

"You're coming with me," she said. "We're not splitting up. That's the way every horror movie starts. People split up and they get killed off."

She smiled, trying to joke. I shook my head.

"I can't leave him like that," I said, nodding toward the window. "Not all by himself."

"We don't have much choice, Hattie. You need to eat and you need to get cleaned up. We'll get back here as quick as we can. Come on. The longer we sit here, the longer he has to suffer. Maybe we can find a vet. What else can we do?"

I put my head against the window. The coolness felt good on my forehead and spread down to my nose.

"I'm at least going to throw a blanket on him."

I jumped out and grabbed a blanket from the back. I took my time walking through the gate and then across the meadow. The sun had turned the sky aluminum gray. I clucked my tongue and told Speed where I was. I fluffed the blanket over my forearm to figure out how I could toss it evenly over him. I stood away from his hooves. Then I shot the blanket out in a swirl and tried to settle it on him.

Astonishingly, he lifted. The blanket must have frightened him, or something must have snapped inside him, but he rolled quickly and got his front legs under him. Then his back legs twisted and dug to get under him, and in a big heave he rocked onto his feet. He passed wind in a long, horrible trombone slide, and his feet threatened to glass out from under him. I shouted for Delores but she had already seen. She clambered through the gate and came sliding up on the icy grass.

"Who's that good-looking boy?" she yelled, her voice

going up and crazy, her steps bringing her close enough to pat him. "Who is he?"

"I can't believe it," I said, and I couldn't.

"He's the best. He's the absolute best."

"He still looks like sin," I said. "He's weak."

"Let's load him and take him into town. We'll give him some hay, and maybe we can find some of those alfalfa pellets Julie talked about. Some vitamins or whatever."

"We need to get him into a barn," I said.

"Well, we can figure it all out. He's up, that's the main thing. He might have just been sleeping. Horses do nutty things."

I put my arms around Speed's neck. His head hung low as if he didn't have the strength to lift it. I kissed him. I kissed him ten times.

"He's okay, Hattie," Delores said, running her hand on his back. "He's as okay as he's been these last few days."

"Did you mean what you were saying about a gun?" I asked her. "I need to know."

"People use a twenty-two," she said, her voice steady and calm. "I've seen it done once. Some people pay for a vet to give them barbiturates, but I'm not sure that's any easier. A gun is quicker, and a horse won't know a thing. My uncle

Willy always said it was the best death in the world for a horse. No suffering. Just gone."

"I'm not ready for that yet," I said.

"I'm not suggesting it. What I'm saying is his condition probably hasn't changed all that much. He was just down for the count. He's been standing a long time on the trip. Maybe he just needed to rest for a while. He came right up when you threw that blanket on him."

I nodded. He did.

"Where?" I asked.

"Where what?"

"Where does the gun go?"

She looked away.

"You hold it perpendicular to the forehead and you put it in the center of an X that runs from the left ear to the right eye."

"You looked it up," I said. "Before we even started, you looked it up."

She nodded.

"And you figured it might come to that?" I asked.

"That's not true," she said. "I saw it done once, like I said. I checked it as a preventive. You know, just in case. I was on Google."

I kept my arms around Speed. We stood for a little while

without talking. The sun kept building and shoving light into the ice and bringing out colors.

WE STOPPED AT A PLACE CALLED PIGLETS.

On a big yellow sign with a neon waitress carrying a tray on her shoulder, the restaurant advertised a breakfast for $9.95, all you can eat. We parked close enough so that we could watch Speed in the trailer. He shifted his weight as we stopped. Delores glanced at the mirror once, fluffed her hair, then came around to my side.

"Bring a change of clothes," she reminded me. "You look like you've been made into sausage."

"Okay," I said.

"We can get the buffet and eat our brains out."

I nodded. I turned around and checked on Speed. He looked stable, his long head held in a better position than before. I told him he was a good boy, then grabbed my small bag containing a new T-shirt and my toiletries and followed Delores inside.

A hostess who was about our age had trouble keeping her eyes off my bloody nose. Her name tag said *Florence*. She stood behind a lectern that appeared to be held up by two chubby pigs. The pigs smiled more than she did. She looked down at a book on her hostess stand when we stood in front of her. Delores told her a table for two. Florence didn't acknowledge us for a second. Delores cast a quick look around. The restaurant was far from crowded. Delores looked at me and crossed her eyes.

"Two?" Florence asked after an awkward moment.

Delores nodded. I knew if she hadn't been so hungry she would have told Florence to suck an egg.

I scooted by them both and went to the ladies' room. It was a big room, fronted with tile. The pig motif danced its way in from the front of the restaurant. Girl pigs in dresses and tutus peeked out from behind the mirrors. They looked coy and silly, like piggy perverts who wanted to cover up their staring by nutty cheeriness. The tile made everything noisy and cold. A hand dryer hummed all by itself on the far wall, as if someone couldn't stand the racket any longer and ran away. Someone occupied the far stall. Maybe they had turned on the hand dryer for white noise.

I stopped at the first sink and felt a little shock at the condition of my face. Speed had knocked me a good one. Blood had dried along my cheeks and down on my neck. Blood clotted my right nostril. My coat had the worst of it; blood went down next to my zipper in a red band, a tiny river swirling back and forth as it went. I put my bag onto a small shelf above the sinks just as the woman in the stall stepped out. She flushed and let the door swing back too far. She had a big shape, round and thick, and she wore painter pants and a navy peacoat. She appeared to be midthirties. Her eyes darted at mine, and I saw the blood register. It took me a moment to see it as she must have seen it—a domestic violence thing, a girl quivering in a restroom—and thinking it somehow gave her permission to speak.

"You okay?" she asked, stepping to the sink farthest down the row. "You need any help?"

She waited to turn on her faucets. She held her hands up a little like a TV doctor waiting to scrub up.

"I'm fine," I said. "An accident."

"You're sure?" she asked.

She looked at me.

"A horse," I said.

She nodded and slowly turned on the faucets. She washed her hands, pumping the soap a couple extra times. Meanwhile, I took off my jacket. I hung it on a stall door, then bent and cleaned my face. The water felt good, but whenever my hands brushed my face, it hurt. I ladled water toward my cheeks and nose for a long time. I felt shaky and tired and hungry. When I looked again at my face, most of the blood had disappeared. The woman, though, still studied me.

"Nobody rides horses this time of year," she said, hitting the hand dryer with her elbow, then shoving her hands under the air. "At least I don't think they do."

"It was a horse," I said. "I appreciate your concern, but it was a horse."

She made a little pout with her face, then left. I slipped off my shirt and dug through my bag for something clean to wear. I pulled my SPAM T-shirt over my head and then spent a few minutes cleaning my jeans with rolled-up toilet paper and soap and water. Afterward I stood so the hand dryer could dry my pants. The hot air made me drowsy. An old woman came in, stared at me, shook her head, then ducked into the stall where the other woman had been.

When I found Delores seated in a booth, she already had three plates in front of her. I slid in across from her.

"How's Speed?" I asked, looking out.

His tail flicked. I watched the trailer shift a little in response to his weight change.

"He's okay," she said. "I've been watching him. He's moving around in there, anyway."

She nodded at me.

"You look better," she said. "You were gruesome there for a while."

"I feel better."

"I couldn't wait to eat," she said, her fingers unwrapping a butter pat. "Sorry. But you can get whatever you want. The waitress asked if I wanted coffee, but I said we'd have tea. Is that okay?"

She buttered a piece of raisin toast. The sound of the knife going over the bread reminded me of the sleet the night before, the frozen water hitting the truck roof and the pin oak and the gate.

"I'll always remember that ride last night," Delores said. "That was worth the whole trip right there. That's a good memory."

"Are we to Blue Earth yet?" I asked.

"No," she said, taking a big bite of toast. "I don't think so. What's your obsession with Blue Earth?"

"It's where they say the sky opens up like it does out West."

"Who said?"

"I don't know," I said. "People, I guess. I've always wanted to see it."

"I'm the one who told you, you weirdo. Jackie, that hippie girl I used to work with, she told me. She used to come out here all the time."

"So, mystery solved. You told me. It just feels like maybe it would be a cliff or something, or a place where one kind of sky gave way to another. I don't know. It got into my imagination somehow."

"Let's try to spend the night in Blue Earth," she said. "We got a late start anyway now. We could use the rest, and so could Speed. And we can look into getting him some vitamin supplements."

I nodded. I watched Speed's tail flick out and over the back gate. Then it pulled back in again. For a minute or two I didn't move. I felt glassy and quiet and warm sitting in the sunlight that came through the window. I'm not sure why, but an old song came into my head, and it was so clear, it caught my breath. It was called "Stewball," and my father had taught it to me when I was a little girl. A folk group named Peter, Paul and Mary used to sing it in three-part harmony. Dad played it off a vinyl record player, which he never did except when he felt good and happy and maybe a little drunk. Mom always left the room when he pulled out old records—Cat Stevens and early James Taylor and Judy Collins—because she said it turned him into a sentimental slob and it made him think of earlier days, and she couldn't stand watching him yearn for a past that wasn't so great anyway. He knew all the songs, even which groove the stylus needed to hit to play which song, and he drank Pabst Blue Ribbons and sang.

"Stewball" was a ballad about longing and lost lives, about putting your money on the wrong horse, but I loved it because in one verse Stewball, who wasn't supposed to win but did anyway, "came a-prancing and a-dancing, my noble Stewball." Dad knew I loved it for the horse stuff and when that bit about Stewball crackled off the vinyl he used to whirr up his arms like horse legs and make a nickering sound. Our secret, Stewball. Our noble, Stewball.

WE STOPPED FOR THE NIGHT AT AN ECONO LODGE OUTSIDE of Blue Earth, Minnesota. It took us a long time to negotiate a deal with the desk clerk—a thin, coat-hanger woman with gray hair, wearing a Western shirt with white swirls across her collarbones—to let Speed graze on grass behind the buildings. The only reason she agreed, she said, was that the Ak-Sar-Ben's River City Rodeo was in town, and she had more cowboys and rodeo people around than anyone knew what to do with. It wasn't the first time people had asked to put a horse onto her grass.

"He pulls loose and gets into traffic, don't go blaming me," she said, her eyeglasses glinting in the fluorescent light.

"We won't," Delores promised.

"I mean it," she said. "Not a word."

With the key in hand, we drove the trailer around back and eased Speed onto a half acre of scrubby brush at the rear of the building. I tethered him out while Delores gave him some hay from the trailer. He shook a little inside his skin and didn't look completely steady on his legs. Delores chucked his chin up and stood for a while looking him over. Speed smelled good and clean after I brushed out a few flecks of manure from his tail, but he still seemed baggy inside, like something had begun to drain away.

"You'll be okay here, Speedy," Delores said. "You just settle down for a while."

"He's soft-feeling," I said. "I don't like it."

"What's that mean, 'soft-feeling'?" she asked, still inspecting him.

"I don't know," I said. "It feels like something is changing in him."

"You can't worry about him so much, Hattie," she said. "He's come all this way. He's going to do what he's going to do. All the worrying in the world won't change a thing."

Still, we fussed over him a little longer. The grass around him looked tired of summer. He picked at the hay Delores carried from the trailer. The swish of hay rubbing together reminded me of barns and late afternoons. If I was honest, though, I couldn't say he looked much different from how he always looked. He was just an old horse. I stepped back and examined him. Thoughts didn't stay pinned down long enough for me to make sense of them. Looking at Speed was like looking at fresh paint on a wall. For a second you thought he looked one way. Then the light changed, or the paint sank deeper into the drywall, and something different caught your eye.

"Did she say 'rodeo'?" I asked Delores as I came up to join her by Speed's head.

"She did indeed," Delores said, smiling at me. "Find a rodeo, you find a cowboy."

"That's all we need."

"When in Blue Earth," she said, "flirt with cowboys. I say we check it out."

"Rodeos are horrible to horses," I said. "And you know it."

"Not completely. Nothing is quite as black-and-white as you like to make it, Hattie."

"They use gelding straps to make the horses buck. Bulls, too."

"I'm not stupid," she said. "I know that."

"Then don't support rodeos."

"I've never been to a rodeo. How do I know what I think about them until I've visited one?"

"You know you don't like raw potato sandwiches and you've never had one of those."

"What in the world is a raw potato sandwich?"

"It's a metaphor, you cheese bag."

"Hattie, what are you getting all huffy for? I just want to see a rodeo. You can't stay out here all night and hold Speed's hand."

"He doesn't have hands," I said, feeling feisty for no reason.

"Still," she said.

We left it at that for the time being. We finished with Speed and then drove back around the motel until we spotted room 6 along the ground level. We parked in front of it. I noticed as we climbed out that we weren't the only horse trailer in the parking lot. I counted six horse trailers and one large livestock trailer that said BOB'S BIG BAD BOYS across the side. Underneath the big sign a smaller script said BUCKING BRAHMA BULLS.

As soon as we swung open the door to the room, Delores ran in and fell onto the far bed.

"Mine!" she said.

"You can have it. I don't care."

"Does it feel good to be inside or what?"

"It feels good," I admitted, "but don't get too accustomed to it. We've got a ways to go."

"We can make it in a day or two, you said," Delores said, fluffing the pillows against the headboard. "Stop worrying. Our money situation is still good, isn't it?"

"Once we leave Speed somewhere, we still have to make it home. Or whatever."

"Maybe," Delores said, "but meanwhile we have a town full of cowboys."

She jumped up, grabbed the remote control, and shot the TV on.

"You take first shower," she said to me. "You smell like a gopher."

"Who's lying in her bed smelling like a horse?"

Delores smooshed her shoulders around. She raised her top lip in a silly, mocking grin. She made a whinnying sound.

"I like horses," she said, her attention on the television. "Oh, look, Oprah!"

I went out to the truck and grabbed my backpack. I fished out my toiletry bag and went back into the room and headed for the bathroom. It shocked me a little to see what I looked like. My hair stuck out in ten directions and my eyes looked tired and punk. The bruises on my face had simmered down, but they still made me wince when I touched them. I stripped off my sweater, then my shirt, then my bra. I turned the water on in the shower to let it run hot. I piled my jeans on the other dirty clothes, stepped out of my underwear, then climbed into the shower. The water came too hot for a second, so I turned it down, but finally it hit me exactly right. It felt better than just about anything I could remember. I turned and let it run over me for a long time. After five or ten minutes, I shampooed my hair with Suave raspberry and conditioned it afterward. I grabbed my nail clippers out of my toiletry bag and spent a few minutes giving myself a pedicure. Then I did my fingernails. By the time I finished the water had turned lukewarm.

I tucked a towel around me and started to go out, but stopped when I heard voices.

I leaned my head out and saw Delores talking to someone at the front door.

"Delores?" I called.

She looked over her shoulder, raised her eyebrows to tell me to give her a second, then turned around again.

"Okay," she said. "Thank you. See you in a little while. . . . Right. Okay."

She closed the door.

"Cowboys," she whispered. "Cute freaking cowboys."

"Who?" I asked, stepping out of the bathroom.

I felt annoyed and wasn't sure why.

"Two guys," she said, "and they're about our age. They saw us come in and they saw our license plates, and they have tickets to the rodeo tonight."

She pronounced "rodeo" as ro-de-Ohhh.

"Geez," I said, "you work fast. You are such a little slut."

"I didn't do anything!" she said, nearly squealing. "They just showed up. I thought it was the manager coming to see us about Speed."

"So what did you say?"

"I said we'd love to go."

She smiled at me. Then she started dancing. It was a dance I'd seen her do a thousand times. It was ridiculous, but I couldn't help laughing. She ran over and grabbed my hands and made me dance too. She went spastic eventually, the way she always does, and she jumped from bed to bed like a maniac, nearly knocking herself out on the ceiling once. She chanted, "Cowboy nookie. We're going to get some cowboy nookie."

"What time?" I managed to ask when she'd calmed down.

She bounced down onto the bed and fell against the pillows.

"Seven-thirty."

"I want to do some laundry."

"We don't have anything to wear. Maybe we should go as SPAM twins, wear our new T-shirts. SPAM dates."

"Sure, Delores, we need to dress up for two cowboys in Blue Earth."

"They're cute, I'm telling you."

"What are their names?" I asked, stepping into a clean pair of underwear I grabbed from my bag.

"Drew was one of them, but I don't remember which one. And I didn't catch the other name."

"This could be a bad idea."

"We're not nuns."

"It just complicates things. Boys always do."

"I could use a little complicating," she said, and wiggled her eyebrows.

"I mean it, Delores. We're a long way from home, and we have Speed to think about."

I didn't like how I sounded even as I said my piece, but I couldn't help it. I saw Delores's face cloud.

"Oh, for Pete's sake, Hattie, quit being such an old woman. We're not going to marry them. We're just going to a rodeo with them. We're women going west."

"I'm doing some laundry," I said, to get off the topic. "If you want to throw anything in, you better get hopping."

"Okay, okay, Ms. Responsibility," she said.

She stood and walked into the bathroom. A few seconds later she came out in a towel with her arms full of dirty clothes.

"Do you think they take their hats off when they kiss you?" she asked as she handed me the laundry. "They must, because otherwise it would poke you right in the forehead."

"THEY ARE TOTALLY HOT," DELORES SAID INTO HER CELL phone, her eyes on the mirror in front of her.

She laughed. She swung the phone up so it looked like a rabbit ear next to her head, and interpreted Paulette's conversation. She had on her Russian SPAM T-shirt, the one with the army marching around and around.

"Paulette says we should marry these guys and become ranch wives and live like prairie women. She says she is totally jealous. She says she has cowboy fantasies all the time. She says she might faint if she kissed a real cowboy at a rodeo."

She swung the phone down again.

"Hattie is being a jerk-face," she told Paulette. "She's turning all Mother Superior on me. All she wants to do is watch some stupid home makeover program. It's so lame."

Phone back up.

"Paulette says you are a foolish, foolish girl. She says carpe cowboy."

Someone knocked.

"They're here," Delores whispered. She ran in place for three steps.

Into the phone: "Okay, I'll call. I will, I promise. . . . Yes. Okay. Not late. . . . I don't know. Who knows? Okay, bye."

Someone knocked again.

"Get the door," Delores said to me.

"You get it."

"Are you going to be like this? You really are?"

"Answer the door."

She looked at herself one last time in the mirror, straightened something in her hair, then pulled open the door partway.

"Howdy," she said, and quickly glanced back at me, cross-eyed.

I heard guys' voices.

"Do we need a coat?" Delores asked. "Is it outside or inside? This is my friend Hattie."

Delores pushed open the door.

Both guys touched the tips of their cowboy hats at the same time. They were as handsome as anything.

"This is Drew, right?" Delores said, pointing to the taller one. "And this is . . . ?"

"I'm Drew," the shorter one said. "And this is Punch. That's what we call him. Well, what everyone calls him. His real name is David."

I stood and went forward and shook their hands.

My eyes met Punch's.

He had gray eyes and a tan cowboy hat. His hair looked brown, a little blond, and his sideburns came down to the bottom of his ears. A faded scar ran over his right eye, and his nose had broken sometime in the past and hadn't healed straight. When his hand covered mine, it was large and strong, and he didn't squeeze my hand so much as cup it and then let it go as he might free a bird. I felt my stomach roll and twist, and I couldn't move my eyes away from his. Drew and Delores saw it, too. It felt like anyone in the world could have seen it.

"How did you all get tickets?" Delores asked, grabbing her jacket. "Are you in the rodeo business?"

"We're with Bob's Brahmas," Drew said. "But the bull riding isn't for another day, so we're just spectators tonight."

"Do you ride the bulls?" I asked.

"No one rides a bull," Drew said, and smiled. "People just try to stay alive on a bull. But he rides a little."

He pointed to Punch.

"And what's the name Punch all about?" I asked.

"That's how he broke his nose," Drew said. "Tell them, Punch."

"Maybe later," Punch said, and his voice had a nice dusty sound to it. "We should go if we want to see the roping."

I grabbed my barn jacket. Delores and I followed the guys out to an enormous pickup truck with double doors. Drew drove. I climbed into the back. Punch climbed in after me.

THE BACK OF DREW'S HEAD, I DECIDED, LOOKED LIKE A clothes iron—pointed down by his neck and widening up into his skull. He talked more than Punch, and I realized, listening to him, that he had been the impetus behind the date. He explained they had been sitting out in front of their room, listening to one of the older guys talk about a bronco that got loose earlier in the morning, when we happened to pull into the parking lot. They had noticed the New Hampshire plates first, and all of them speculated about the possibility of New Hampshire riders, and the old guy—his name was Herbert—said he didn't know about New Hampshire, but he had gone with rodeos to Boston and it had always surprised him that Easterners seemed to like rodeos as much as the next person. They watched us climb out, and the older guy, Herbert, said that Drew and Punch ought to lasso themselves a pair of runaway fillies, which was meant to be a joke when Drew said it, but it was kind of corny, and no one laughed. When we came back from dropping off Speed, they decided to swing by and invite us, so here we were, all of us going to the rodeo. Drew said the tickets gave us the right to sit up close, and he had another friend, a clown for the bull riding, who could get us free food if we were hungry. He said all this speaking above the radio, which played country and twanged, and Delores nodded at everything, and for a fraction of a second I felt like a little kid again in the backseat of my parents' car, way back before they divorced, and I remembered sitting and listening to my dad talk, all puffy the way Drew did, and the sound of the radio and heater mixing until it soothed me somehow.

Punch reached over and took my hand.

Just like that.

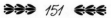

I didn't look at him, but I didn't move my hand from his. I felt such a commotion in my stomach and guts that I thought for a second I might have to put my head down between my knees and breathe steadily.

Delores said, "Blah, blah, blah, blah," and I had no idea what she said, but when she turned around to catch my eye, she flashed down to our hands sitting between us, and she turned right back as though she had seen a snake. But I liked the way my hand felt in his, and I liked his hand. It felt as rough as rope, and dry and quiet. He didn't flex his fingers, or do anything stupid, or try to send me secret messages. He simply held my hand, and it felt like the world had become less empty by his doing it. You wondered why people didn't always hold hands, even if they had just met.

A minute or two later Drew pulled into the parking lot of the Qwest Center, a large, lighted pavilion. He stopped and talked to someone taking tickets, said he was with the bulls, flashed a pass at the guy, then drove forward and around the building. Delores turned again and peeked at our hands while pretending to say something else. Her lips moved, but the words didn't penetrate my head.

"Here we are," Drew said, turning off the engine. "Your first rodeo, ladies."

"Yeehaw," Delores said, and I wished she hadn't.

Drew climbed out. Punch climbed out after Delores, and he let go of my hand, then reached back in and helped me out. I tried to judge what Delores thought of Drew, but I couldn't tell. She and Drew walked ahead of us. I wanted Punch to take my hand again, but he didn't.

"Do you still like the rodeo?" I asked Punch as we walked toward a wide garage door that served as an entrance for people with passes. "I mean, working for it and seeing it all the time."

"Rodeos are pretty fun," Punch said. "I don't much like all the noise, though. I'm not crazy about crowds."

"Me neither."

"I always thought places like New Hampshire were pretty crowded," he said. "Places back East."

"The southern part of the state is a little crowded, but not up north. It's cold, and employment can be tough, so people don't want to live up there. That's the part we're from. I like it fine. It's the prettiest state I've seen."

"You ever seen Wyoming?"

I shook my head.

"We're from Wyoming," he said, and left it at that.

Delores grabbed me as soon as we made it inside. She

said something to Drew about going to the ladies' room. She hooked her arm through my arm and whispered not to look back. We walked past snack bars and ice cream counters, and past two gift shops selling cowboy paraphernalia. One place had a large sign outside promising discounts on Stetson hats. As we walked, buzzers went off, and the crowd yelled at something happening down in the ring. It felt strange to be in such a lighted place when outside it had been dark for more than an hour.

"Was he holding your hand?" she asked me, her head still straight ahead.

"Yes."

"OMG," she said. "And Drew is a weirdo. Did you hear the music he played on the ride here?"

"What did you expect a guy who works for Bob's Bucking Brahmas to listen to, Delores?"

She grabbed my hand and yanked me into the restroom. As soon as we made it inside, she turned and looked at me. A woman near the sinks yanked a paper towel out of the holder and wiped her face with the towel.

"Do you like him?" Delores asked.

"Punch?"

"Of course, Punch!" she yelped.

"Well, sure. He's nice."

"And unbelievably handsome."

"He's cute," I said.

I stepped over to the mirror above a row of sinks and checked my reflection. Delores stood beside me. She took out some lip gloss and fingered it onto her lips. The woman with the paper towel crumpled it, tossed it into a trash barrel, and left. I looked at my bruises. I wondered why Punch hadn't asked about them.

"Gorgeous is more like it," Delores said. "Punch, I mean. Drew's cute, but he knows it, and that's a turnoff. Plus, he's an opinionated little tumbleweed."

"Tumbleweed?" I asked her. "Where are you coming up with all this cornball stuff? Are you having second thoughts?"

"I'm just here for the rodeo," she said.

"You're acting nutty, Delores."

"I guess it feels strange having people between us after all we've been doing," she said. "It just is."

"I know what you mean," I said, "but we might as well see the rodeo. It's just one night. We'll be gone tomorrow."

"You promise?"

I looked at her, reflection to reflection.

"What's going on, Delores?"

She shrugged. Our eyes stayed on each other's for a little bit. And I knew some sort of spiral had started in her and that she could feel it, too. Maybe Drew had set it off, or maybe seeing me holding hands with Punch had done it, but she had begun to sink, and she couldn't tell me any way but this.

"I'm sorry," she said, looking at me. "I get all crazy. I was thinking this was going to be so great, but now all I can think about is I'm out in Minnesota and I'm at a rodeo with some guy I don't even know, and after this, later on, I don't know where I'm going."

"Do you want to say you got sick?" I asked. "We can make our excuses."

She shook her head.

"I'm going to ask my dad if I can go live with him," she said, her eyes filling. "Just for a while. Just to see something else."

"That could be just the thing for you right now, Delores."

"I know, but then he called and started giving me grief about the trailer and everything, so I don't know. I guess I had talked myself into thinking that was how it would go. I mean, to go visit him. And maybe Drew tonight—well, I get so crazy with ideas, thinking things will happen a certain way, and then when they don't, I'm let down. It takes the wind out of me, Hattie. I keep telling myself not to get too high or low, but you know, when I saw those cowboys, I thought, This is my future, this is the man I'm going to marry. How pathetic is that?"

"Did you want Punch? Is that it?"

"No, he's your age, anyway, and he's all wrapped up in you. I'm not man crazy or anything. It just feels like I'm walking around with a key in my hand, and I keep trying it in different doors and the locks never tumble for me. It sounds ridiculous, I'm sure. I'm sorry. And you're meeting this amazing-looking guy."

Then she really cried. Two older women came in and looked at us, then passed by and went into stalls. I held Delores and let her cry it out. After a while she pushed off my shoulder and bent to the sink and washed her face. "Cowboy up," she whispered, which is what the Red Sox said a few seasons back to get themselves rallied up. She dried her face and hands on paper towels. Delores loved the Red Sox.

"You sure you want to go through with this date?" I said. "We don't owe them anything."

"I'm just being a poop," she said. "We're in Blue Earth, for goodness' sakes, where the western sky meets the eastern horizon."

"That's awkward," I said.

She laughed.

"Drew's cute, right?" she asked, straightening her clothes.

"Sure, he's cute."

"Expectation is the enemy of serenity," she said.

"Where'd you get that?"

"Fortune cookie," she said, yanking me toward the door. "Let's grab some cowboy."

Chapter 7

DREW SHOVED A BIG CHEW OF TOBACCO INTO HIS MOUTH, then lifted his lower lip like a camel and wrapped it over the wad. He made a sucking sound as he did it, as if his saliva had rushed out to meet an old friend. I watched Delores's eyes go wide when she realized what he had done. She looked at me. Then she reached over and grabbed the tobacco out of Drew's hand and squeezed out a pinch and jammed it into her mouth. We were in the grandstands sitting on wooden bleachers. Not many people sat near us. The boys sat on the outside. The seats we were supposed to get down at ground level had been promised to a VIP, it turned out.

"You're a crazy girl," Drew said, and stretched his legs out in front of him.

Punch shook his head. Punch held my hand.

I knew Delores was bored and a little manic. The rodeo didn't end up being quite what we had expected. It had a sawdust ring and a lot of glaring light and constant music punctuating everything that happened. The announcer made a series of jokes we didn't get, or didn't find funny. I couldn't keep my eyes off the gelding straps that made the horses buck, and when the riders bulldogged a bunch of calves, I thought they might break the animals' necks. I didn't like that, and neither did Delores, but we liked the clown who ran in and out at various times to amuse the audience. The clown's name was Cecile, and he had a funny way, his pants droopy and his hat tilted on his head. He wore sneakers instead of big clown shoes. He needed the sneakers to run from bulls and to dodge in when a cowboy got in trouble. His real name, Drew told us, was Harry, but Cecile was his clown name. Clowns got gored, too, Drew said, and kicked and beat, but a good clown saved lives, and Cecile was a good one even if he had gotten a little older and hard of hearing.

Delores and I liked the barrel racing, where women riders worked their way around a cloverleaf course and made the horse maneuver in tight circles and bends. Punch and Drew said barrel racing counted as the stupidest, most annoying event in any rodeo, and that it was put on for wives who used to be bored while their men participated in the rougher sports. When Delores and I heard that, we played up our enjoyment of the barrel riding because we liked being exotic to these boys and we liked seeing women doing something active. We were Easterners, not like the typical Western girls they dated, and we kept drawing the line, bright and wide, so they would see it.

Being exotic is probably what made Delores take a dip of tobacco.

"How is it?" I asked her.

"It doesn't stay together," she said, her voice working around her open mouth. "I thought it formed into a chunk or something. But it's like chewing rubber bands."

"You keep it in your lip," Drew said, "but don't swallow the juices or you'll be as sick as Jupiter."

"I want it out," Delores said.

Drew handed her an empty soda cup. Delores yakked it up like a cat frowning out a hair ball. She used her index finger to get it all out. Then she grabbed a napkin from me and licked her tongue on it.

"'Gross' does not begin to cover it," she said.

Drew smiled.

"You two just aren't rodeo fans," he said, taking up a theme we had already covered. "You got to stop thinking about it and just enjoy it."

"What is it like to ride a bull?" I asked Punch.

"Isn't much fun," Punch said, his eyes on a Ford F-250 that a local dealership had driven into the ring as a way of advertising deals. The pickup was black and had a bed liner and glistening hubcaps. Someone had buffed it like crazy. A truck never looked better.

"Then why do you do it?" I asked.

"Boys do some stupid things," he said. "That's the definition of 'boys.'"

"But what is it like?" I asked, my shoulder against his, my hand in his. I'd already decided I wanted to kiss him before the night was over.

"It's a lot of yanking on your arm," he said, lowering his voice so only I could hear. "When you tie in, you hook your arm in, and when the bull starts to go, it's your shoulder that gets it worst at first. Then after a while the whole world shrinks to the space right above the bull's head. If it has horns—blunted, you know—then you see everything as the bull sees it, and sometimes your mind goes away completely and you just ride by instinct. I don't know. Bulls don't treat you right."

"Is it the danger you like?"

He pursed his lips.

"Never really thought of it that way," he said. "Just a thing to ride, I guess. And a little prize money from time to time."

His hand covered my hand as simply as a glove.

"You know," Drew said, "we don't have to stay. We could get out of here if you two want to. Can't say Punch and I haven't seen enough rodeos in our days."

"To go where?" Delores asked, apparently okay with taking off.

"We could go get some food."

"What do you say, Hattie?" Delores asked, turning to me.

"I'm ready," I said.

"There's a Chinese place in town that's good," Punch said. "Some of the older guys go there."

A loud whoop marked the end of the advertisement for the Ford F-250. We stood. Punch held my hand and led me out. I liked seeing his profile under the cowboy hat.

"WHAT I WANT TO KNOW," DELORES SAID, A BOWL OF chicken lo mein in front of her, her fork dragging noodles upward, "is how come there is a Chinese restaurant in every town in the country. I mean, you can't tell me some Chinese family in some small village in China decides one day to open a restaurant in Blue Earth, Minnesota. That doesn't make sense. Who tells them where to go? And how come they don't end up having maybe five restaurants in the same little town?"

"They do sometimes," Drew said, biting into a dumpling.

Delores shook her head.

"Someone has to be like the air traffic controller. Right? Someone has to say, 'You open a restaurant in New Hampshire, and you other folks open one in Minnesota.' I mean, does someone do a demographic check to see if the population is sufficient to support the restaurant? How does it all work?"

"So you think," Drew said, putting down his dumpling and shaking soy sauce onto it, "that a Chinese guy sits somewhere, and he has a map of the United States and he puts pins into different towns when a restaurant goes in? Is that what you're claiming?"

"I don't know what I'm saying," Delores said. "I'm just saying."

"Someone said Ray Kroc used to fly around the country and look down and figure out places to put McDonald's outlets," Punch said.

"So maybe a Chinese guy flies around," I said, trying to

push the conversation in a different direction. Delores and Drew could go round and round.

"The McDonald brothers are from New Hampshire," Delores said. "McDonald's is New Hampshire's gift to the world. Isn't that just perfect?"

Before Drew answered, the waitress came to fill our water glasses and check if we needed anything. She was a short middle-aged Chinese woman who took small steps. To start the meal, she had handed out radishes carved into swans and a wallet-sized menu with the name Han Se Chinese Restaurant on the front. Her name tag said *Uh*. I didn't know if that was a misspelling or what.

Punch held his water glass up to be filled. He thanked her. He had ordered orange chicken. His hat hung on the back of his chair. His hair was long and wavy and the color of pine shavings. I liked the way his jaw muscles flexed when he ate. Delores declined water, and so did Drew. I asked Uh to fill up mine. The food tasted spicy and strong.

"So what are you all doing out here anyway?" Drew asked when the waitress had left. "What's all this stuff about a horse?"

"We are taking a horse out west," Delores said.

"Delivering it?" Punch asked, interested.

"In a manner of speaking," I said. "We stole it."

"You stole a horse?" Punch asked.

He took a sip of water.

"I stole it from a place I worked," I said. "They planned to put him down."

"So you took him?" Drew asked. "Just like that?"

I shrugged.

"Where are you going to take him?" Punch asked.

"We thought we'd put him out on a range somewhere," I said. "Where he can be a horse."

"What's he now if he's not a horse?" Drew asked, starting to laugh.

"I mean so he can live like a horse should live," I said. "Be free for a little while."

"I see," Punch said, and I believed he did.

"So let me get this straight," Drew said, setting down his fork and lifting his water. "You stole a horse to bring it out here and let it go? Is that it, more or less?"

"You don't understand anything," Delores said.

"But is that what you're saying?" Drew insisted.

"You can reduce anything," Delores said, "and if you reduce it enough it sounds silly."

Drew smiled and shook his head. He picked up his fork again and starting pulling at more noodles.

"I know a place," Punch said, looking at me, then at Delores. "Not far from here, either."

"Where?" I asked.

"An old rodeo guy named Fry. He's got a big hunk of land outside of town here, and he lets some horses range over it. He's got a deal worked out with a rodeo. The PETA people are always watching how the animals are treated, so when they get too old, at least some of them, they go out to Fry's. He'd let your horse go free out there."

I looked at Delores. I felt my heart beating hard.

"Speed's been wobbly lately. He went down the other day and had trouble getting back up," I said. "That's his name, Speed."

"Well, sorry to say, it might be his time," Punch said. "I could take a look at him. I grew up around horses."

I felt my throat close off a little. I wondered, looking at Delores and watching Drew eat, if maybe everyone all the way along had thought Speed was better off dead. The Fergusons had thought so, and so had my mom, and even Delores, in her way, hadn't jumped in to defend Speed all the way across. Maybe I was being paranoid, I couldn't tell, but it hit me that perhaps people had humored me and that I had been foolish enough, and blind enough, to imagine they agreed. Maybe

Speed had always been my issue. Delores cared about him, but she wanted to go west, and Speed provided an excuse for the trip. I put down my fork and drank some water. I felt dizzy and light-headed.

"You should bring old Woody over," Drew said, half to us, half to Punch. "He's the rodeo vet and a friend of ours. He could tell you in no time how sound your horse might be. There's not a thing that man doesn't know about horses."

"I could do that," Punch said to me. "He's a good guy, and he'd help you out."

I nodded.

I lost my appetite and felt strange and grindy down in my guts. The guys ate awhile longer, but soon Uh came back with a check. Delores paid, which seemed right because the guys had treated us to the rodeo, and they left a tip. We took four fortune cookies from a big bowl near the front of the restaurant. Delores broke hers open right away, and it said *You must watch the birds to know when the seed is sown.* Punch read his, and I didn't catch it all. Then Drew made us all listen while he said "*'A wise man carries a baby inside him all his life.'*" I stuck mine into my pocket without opening it. I wasn't being secretive or dramatic. I understood that if it said anything possibly related to Speed, I'd cry like a big blubber-puss, and I didn't want to do that in front of two cowboys.

When we got back to the motel, I told Delores I wanted to check on Speed, and Punch agreed to go with me. I grabbed a headlamp from our room, and Drew and Delores had a little good-night moment. They hadn't hit it off, exactly, and neither one of them felt like faking it, but they hugged quickly, thanked each other, and called it a night. Delores looked dead at me as I left with Punch. She didn't have to say anything.

PUNCH KISSED ME BEFORE WE MADE IT AROUND BACK.

He kissed me long and hard, pushing me against a wall between two doors. He tasted a little like Chinese food, and a little like minty tea, and his body felt as long and as tough as a streetlamp pole. I kissed him back. I had been kissed by boys before a couple times, but never anyone like Punch, never in Minnesota, never by someone I had known only a couple of hours. When he broke away, he grabbed my hand and pulled me free of the wall, and he said he had wanted to kiss me all night, sorry, was it okay, because his mother had brought him up to be a gentleman, and he didn't mean to press me.

"It was fine," I said. "I wanted to kiss you, too."

He smiled.

"Let's go look at your horse," he said.

I said a little prayer of thanks when I saw Speed picking

at hay near the line of bushes. Punch took my hand as we walked over, and I handed him the headlamp so he could use it to inspect Speed. Almost instantly I saw that Punch understood horses. He was calm to begin with, but as he put his hand on Speed, his manner became full and easy, like patting down a comforter, and he talked in a low, cadenced voice that took the tension out of my shoulders. Punch shined the headlamp down from above so he could see Speed's face and eyes. Then he walked under Speed's muzzle and ran his hand along the horse's body.

"Big guy," he said when he was halfway down Speed's flank.

"Sixteen and a half hands," I said. "He's been a fair pony, if you know what I mean. He gave rides."

"Couple dollars a ride," Punch said. "I know."

"How does he look to you?"

Punch shrugged. The circuit between his brain and his lips took its time, I realized. He didn't blurt things out, which was something I admired in him.

"Of course," he said eventually, "it's hard to tell anything in this light. He looks dry and drawn. That might just be the trailer ride. He seems a little edgy, maybe, like he's not feeling all here. This guy Woody claims a horse can go away in its mind when it needs to. That's how your Speed seems to me."

"You think he's done?" I asked, trying to sound casual but feeling my throat tighten.

"I don't know a thing like that, Hattie," Punch said. "Let me bring Woody over. You know, one way or the other you could put him out on Fry's land and let him be a free horse for a couple days. Then if he doesn't seem to thrive, well, you can take care of things. If he does, then you're all set."

I looked at him and nodded. It was the best plan, given how things had tumbled. He grabbed my hands and pulled me into him, but instead of hugging me he lifted me up right onto Speed. I had to swing my leg up to get it over, but Speed didn't seem to mind. Even after he let go of me, I felt Punch's hands under my arms, the pressure like the rubber ends of crutches up in my armpits.

"There's a good-looking boy," Punch said. "That's a horse."

"He was pretty in his day," I said, to my surprise not feeling self-conscious around Punch.

"I can see that," Punch said, and took Speed by the halter and walked him in a circle. Punch studied him and told me to just walk him forward a little. Punch stepped back and shined the light on Speed's legs and hooves, trying to see his gait. Punch squatted down and didn't move for a while. I rubbed Speed's neck and shoulders. It felt amazing to be on Speed's back, amazing to have a cowboy squatting on the ground in front of me, watching.

"You see anything?" I asked.

"I see a good-looking girl on a nice horse," he said.

"I mean about the horse," I said.

Punch stood and shrugged.

"He's an old horse," Punch said. "I can't tell how sick he is, but I'll be honest with you, Hattie. I don't like his chances of making it through a winter around here. Not pastured. If you could keep him in a barn somehow, well, he might stand a chance. But even then I wouldn't be sure. How old did you say he is?"

"We don't really know," I said. "Old, though."

Punch stepped forward and lifted Speed's head. He fanned back Speed's gums and inspected the horse's mouth. I knew he was examining the wear on the teeth. Anyone who tried to guess a horse's age did that. When he finished, he walked to Speed's side and held up his hands to me. I swung my leg over Speed's back and slid off into Punch's arms. He eased the drop and set me on my feet. He had strong hands.

I moved back to Speed's head.

"I can get Woody to come over," Punch said, "but I'm not sure how much he can add. I'm not claiming to be the last word on horses, but he just looks old to me, Hattie. I'm sorry to say it."

"Still," I said.

Punch didn't say anything. I kept my hands busy on Speed's neck and ears.

"Why this horse?" Punch asked quietly.

I shrugged.

"There's got to be a reason," Punch said. "Maybe you can't say. I had a horse, not my first one but the second one. He wasn't even as good as the first one, but I loved that horse. I don't know why. He just got to me like some horses do."

"I think," I said, my forehead close to Speed's, "Speed gets to me because he never fought back. Whatever anyone wanted from him, he gave. And he didn't complain and he did it year after year. I don't know. Somewhere along the line someone has to acknowledge that. He was a gentle, kind creature and he deserves a rest. I wanted him to be a horse, but maybe in some way he was more of a horse than a thousand stallions out on a prairie. Think of all the children he carried on his back, the joy he gave them, and he never asked for anything himself. He never would have thought to ask for anything, so I have to ask for him. Day in, day out, he showed patience to everyone. I love him for that. He taught me that."

I couldn't look at Punch. He didn't say anything anyway. He just took one of my hands and held it.

Chapter 8

THE TELEVISION WAS STILL ON WHEN I GOT BACK TO OUR room. It was late, probably around one. Delores was asleep, her head turned away from the television and the small desk lamp that sat on the bedside table between our beds. A half-empty bag of Cheetos sat with its mouth open, a few orange puffs, like fluffy molars, escaped onto the spread beside her. Her phone lay next to the Cheetos.

I slipped into the bathroom, brushed my teeth, washed my face, and then tiptoed back out. I pulled down the top blanket and slid into the other bed. It felt good to be in clean sheets, to be in a bed with a light nearby and a bathroom handy if I wanted it. My body sunk into the mattress, and I felt a comfortable release. I clicked off the bedside lamp.

"So do they?" Delores asked when the light went out, her voice smoky with sleep.

"Do what?" I asked. "I'm sorry. I didn't mean to wake you."

"Do they kiss with their hats on?" she said. "Paulette wants to know as bad as I do."

"Sometimes," I said.

Her voice suddenly got stronger. "You tell me every detail, Ms. Hattie Wyatt, or I'm going to come over there and do something horrible. I'm too sleepy to think of what, but you tell me."

"We just kissed and talked," I said.

"He's freaking gorgeous," Delores said. "I told Paulette. He may be the most handsome boy I ever saw."

I didn't know what to say to that, so I didn't say anything.

"Where?" she asked.

"Where what?"

"Where did you go?"

"We sat in his truck. In Drew's truck."

"Ooooo la la."

"Don't make me feel weird about it," I said. "We talked mostly."

"Who's doing that? I'm jealous. So is Paulette. She wants you to call her as soon as you get in."

"I'll tell her I didn't come in until the morning."

"You'll give her a heart attack."

"Sorry about Drew."

"He's too much like me," she said, and laughed quietly.

I heard the Cheetos bag move.

"Are you eating?" I asked.

"Nawwww," she said, her mouth full.

"You hog."

The bag suddenly landed on the bed beside me. I fished around for it until I found the open end. I had a handful and then threw them back to her. My stomach felt good and giddy.

"Do you like him?" she asked after she swallowed.

I heard her scoop out more.

"Yes, I do," I said.

"Not too much, I hope."

I ate the Cheetos.

"Be careful, sweetie," she said. "We're a long way from home."

"I will be."

"Sure you will, you cowboy wrangler."

"Give back the Cheetos."

I heard the bag ruffle, then land next to me. A little light

came in from outside, enough to make the bag look like a live thing as it flew through the air.

"I called my dad," Delores said. "I asked if I could stay with him."

I raised up onto my elbow. I could just make out her outline in bed.

"What did he say?"

"He said I could."

"And how did he sound?"

"Sincere, actually."

"That's wonderful, Delores."

"I'd rather kiss a cowboy."

"But that's big news. That's really big. Did you two talk at all?"

"Sort of. He kind of apologized for going ape about us taking the horse. And he said he always thought about me, and he said stories always have two sides. I guess he meant that Mom always said he just sort of ran off, but he was trying to say something different. He's got an apartment over his garage. It's small and not very fancy, but I could set up there for a while. He said we could get to know each other and see how it went."

"I'm really glad for you, Delores," I said.

"I guess I won't be coming back east with you."

"I kind of knew you wouldn't. Down in my bones, I knew it."

"He's going down to Mexico in a month or so when the weather gets bad. An annual trip, he said. He's got a girlfriend there."

"It'll work out," I said. "It already has."

"We'll still get Speed all set," she said. "Don't worry about that."

"I'm not worried," I said. "Everything is going to be all right for all of us."

Then no one talked for a while. I thought Delores had dropped off. I lay in bed thinking how a day could change things, how a single phone call could change the whole direction of your life. I ran my tongue over the orange silt of the Cheetos on my teeth. A few quick images of Punch came to me, but I didn't want them right then. They still burned and were too sharp. I needed to let them quiet down and become simple and still. I needed to back up a few steps, to let a little time go by.

"I'm going to live in Oregon," Delores whispered. "It's a whole new start."

"I'm happy for you."

Then suddenly she had slipped out of her bed and her arms came around me. She hugged me hard, and I could tell she had started to let go of something. Call it fear, or the misgivings she had earlier in the night, but she cried for a few seconds and squeezed me so tight I couldn't move.

"No one's ever been a better friend than you," she whispered. "Thank you for putting up with me. Thank you, Hattie."

"You're welcome," I said. "You've been good to me, too."

She squeezed me once more. Then she climbed back into her bed.

"Quit hogging the Cheetos," she said a few seconds later.

She laughed hard at her own joke, but for a while it sounded like tears and laughing mixed.

"THIS IS PRETTY," DELORES SAID, HER HANDS AT TWO AND ten on the steering wheel, her eyes scouting over the rolling countryside. "It's kind of like what we envisioned for him."

"And it's a perfect day," I said, the map Punch had drawn for us spread on my lap. "It doesn't get better than this."

"You sure this guy is expecting us?"

"Punch said he set it up. We can camp on his land for a little to see how Speed does. He's got some mustangs out here. Punch said he gets a supplement from the Department of the Interior to let them roam around."

"We should have gotten more supplies if we're camping. I'm always hungry these days."

"Maybe you're pregnant."

"You'd have to have a date to be pregnant."

"You had a date with Drew."

"If you call that a date."

I shrugged. I couldn't take my eyes off the land. It didn't look as green as New England, but the sky had opened wide. Great white clouds migrated across the blue. The sun cut around the clouds and stitched out shadows on the hillsides. The land looked like a blanket someone had spread on a bed, not the last fluff, but the time before the last shake when you finally get the blanket more or less flat on the bed. It looked as if someone had shaken the mountains out of the land, but hadn't gotten rid of everything. A stream crackled over the northern end of the drive, and we passed over water on a wooden bridge before ducking down into some sort of valley. The stream ran away from us, but we saw trees following down the hill, and far away it bent east again and scattered into pods of trees without any meaning. A barbed wire fence circled everything.

"This is pretty," Delores said again. "This is a good possibility. Old Speedy is going to like it here."

"Do you believe this sky?" I asked, sounding a little like a broken record. "You believe it can look like this?"

"It's way open. And you're in love. That makes everything look better."

"It goes on forever. I didn't know what it would look like, but now I do."

"Blue Earth," Delores said.

Then we saw horses.

I know it sounds crazy, but I saw them in my heart before I saw them on the sloping grade above us. Their hooves made a deep pounding sound, and a second later they appeared. Delores reached over and grabbed my arm and we sat frozen and watched them come. A herd of horses, all stirring up grass and dust and slobber. They ran right at us, flinging themselves along the ground, a few prideful males out on the flanks, ears flexing, tails up, hooves gouging the dirt. No halters, I realized. No anything. They ran naked and pure, a blend of muscle and hair and sound, and I felt my heart lift in my chest and nearly burst. Delores pulled over and jammed the truck into park and jumped out. I did, too. I couldn't help running back to the trailer and yelling for Speed to look, and I bawled like an idiot, my chest heaving and unable to catch air.

"That's who you are," I whispered to Speed. "That's a true

horse." Meanwhile Delores scrambled under the fence lining the road and ran at the horses. She held up her hands as if signaling a touchdown and ran as hard as she could. She tried to gallop, tried to be a horse, for all I knew, but they hardly noticed her. They swirled down the hill, dust lifting to cover them, and they seemed like a dream, some surreal movie effect, but Delores chased them, screaming her head off, laughing, too. In a second they left, disappeared, and Delores stopped and screamed more, yelled and jumped in one spot, wiggled her butt, wiggled everything, pawed at the ground. I reached in and put my hand on Speed.

"That's what you are," I whispered to him. "That's who you are."

"I KNOW WHAT YOU'RE THINKING," FRY SAID, "SO LET'S just say I am *aware* that I have one leg and one arm. Take a good look for a second or two at me. Then we're going to get on with things and that's the finish of it."

Fry looked to be about sixty, and he was large and round and he had obviously been in an accident somewhere down the line. Something had chopped off his left hand and half his forearm. He clumped out of his house, a low, gray ranch house, at the first sound of our truck. He wore his hair long, in an Indian braid down the center of his back, and carried a hoe in his good hand. He used the hoe as a cane.

"Looked enough?" he asked, his voice surprisingly reedy for such a big man. "It makes sense to get it right out in the open rather than having people peeking for the first couple hours. Got caught on a railroad bed, long story, but it had something to do with drink and just being young and stupid. So, now, let's see this horse Punch mentioned."

We went around the rear of the trailer and backed Speed out. He looked tired; some gunk had dammed up in his eyes, and he appeared weepy and stunned. Fry watched us, his weight on the hoe that he hooked under his good arm. He seemed ready to cultivate a garden, only I couldn't see any plants to speak of around the house.

"Well, well, well," Fry said. "All the way out from New Hampshire, you say?"

"He was a carnival horse. Gave rides to kids," Delores said.

She took a flat, no-nonsense tone with him. He seemed to appreciate that.

"It's a lot to ask of an old horse to run in a herd," he said. "His best days are gone by."

"We want him to be free for a while," I said. "You know."

"I don't really 'know,' as you put it," Fry said, shifting the hoe under his arm, "but if that's what you want, you go ahead. You can camp up there by the trees. There's some water there. I'm not promising anything about that horse. If anyone comes by to ask, you pretend you're just camping. I get paid by the horse, at least most of the time, but they don't keep good records. If he starts to suffer, we'll put him down. No ifs, ands, or buts. You agree with those terms?"

I nodded.

"You should have a decent spell of weather. I don't want you up there for long. A couple days, then you be on your way, with the horse or not."

"Yes, sir," Delores said.

"Don't say 'sir' unless you mean it," Fry said. "Nothing could be more insulting."

"If he does okay, he can stay?" I asked, wanting to be sure.

"Makes no difference to me. I've got more acres than I know what to do with. Overwintering is a son of a gun. These horses are on a tight margin in January. You should know that."

"Do you supplement their food?" I asked.

He nodded.

"I like horses," he said. "Don't get me wrong. We feed them, but it's still a long winter in Minnesota."

He pointed again at the line of trees we had seen earlier.

"Up there," he said. "Punch coming out later?"

I nodded.

"I knew his father is how come," he said.

Then he turned around and headed toward the house.

I told Delores to drive the truck up while I walked Speed. I hooked a lead onto him. Delores bounced the truck and trailer up a long hill, heading for a clump of trees at the top. I watched her go, then turned around a couple times to see Speed's gait. He still didn't look good. Even in the middle of a glorious day, he looked like he drew more light into him than he reflected. I tried to think of remedies, things the Fergusons might have done, but I couldn't come up with anything.

By the time we reached the top of the hill, Delores already had the tent spread out on the ground. She moved her arm like a television game-show model to point out how the land stretched around us. We hadn't gained much elevation, but it was enough to crack open a view that went on for miles. I wondered aloud why Fry hadn't built up here, and Delores said the wind would be ferocious all winter, and she was probably right. The trees gave us a sugary shade. I unclipped Speed to let him wander. He walked off a few paces and poked at the grass.

We set up the tent, stuck in our sleeping bags and pads,

and then ate an early lunch of peanut butter and jelly sandwiches. We sat on the tailgate and watched Speed. He looked
handsome walking along the ridgeline, even if he did look
old. We needed to figure a way to get him water. After lunch,
I figured, we could walk him down to the stream.

"We forgot to call Paulette," Delores said, her mouth
working on a sandwich. "She's going to be nutty mad at us."

"It would have been too late to call her, with the time
difference."

"True," Delores said. "When I live in Oregon, you'll have
to call later in your day. You'll be ahead of us."

I nodded.

"I should call home," I said, thinking of the phone.

"I'm sorry you have to travel back alone," Delores said.
"I guess it's unavoidable."

"What are you going to do about the trailer?"

"My dad said he could use it for his ATV. I'm going to
have to pay Cousin Richard."

"I can chip in."

"You didn't take it," she said.

"Still," I said.

"It's one of those things that will probably go away if I
don't bring it up. Cousin Richard is a jackass and everyone
knows it."

Delores fixed us each another half a sandwich. We drank cherry water with it. I'm not sure what Delores thought, but I couldn't quite get my head around the fact that we had come to the end of the trip. We hadn't said it, but this was the last stop for Speed, one way or the other. We both knew that. In a day or two, maybe sooner, Delores was going to drop me at a bus station and she was going west and I was going east.

"What's that poem you say about horses?" Delores asked, her sandwich halfway to her mouth.

"The Shakespeare quote?"

She nodded.

"'He is pure air and fire,'" I said.

Delores repeated it.

"'And the dull elements of earth and water never appear in him,'" I said.

Then Delores.

"'But only in patient stillness while his rider mounts him,'" I went on.

Delores.

"'He is indeed a horse; and all other jades you may call beasts,'" I finished.

She repeated it. Little by little she said it more fluently. I coached her through it. We watched Speed and kept saying the lines together until eventually I couldn't tell her voice from mine.

"'He is pure air and fire; and the dull elements of earth and water never appear in him, but only in patient stillness while his rider mounts him: he is indeed a horse; and all other jades you may call beasts,'" we said.

We were still practicing when Punch pulled up towing a horse trailer. He waved out the window. He had someone else in the truck with him, but I couldn't see who. They pulled around the rough, circular driveway in front of Fry's house. The trailer appeared twice as big as ours.

"You have a boyfriend," Delores said, bumping her shoulder into mine.

"You're full of it."

"Well, why would he be here? And why would he set this all up if he didn't like you?"

"I didn't say he didn't like me. I said he wasn't a boyfriend."

"You're blushing," she said, and I was.

"Just don't be a jerk," I said.

"You should run down the hill and leap into his arms. That would be romantic."

"I stink of peanut butter," I said.

"Punch and Hattie up in a tree . . ."

I whacked her with my shoulder to make her stop. We watched Punch jump out of the truck. An old man with bright white hair climbed out the other side. He waved as if we knew him. I waved back. The old man walked slumped over, the hinge of his belt cranked too tight. He exchanged a word or two with Punch by the truck's nose, then put his hand on Punch's shoulder and went toward the house. Punch turned toward us and headed up the hill.

PUNCH KISSED ME ON THE CHEEK, SWEET AND NICE. HE smelled like horses and straw. He tipped his hat at Delores. Delores smiled. She liked cowboy manners.

"Pretty up here," Punch said, looking around. "You guys all set up?"

"Yes," I said. "We're going to see how Speed does."

"I brought Woody out. The rodeo vet. He had to come out this way to talk to Fry anyway, and he said he'd take a look at your horse."

Something flip-flopped in my stomach.

"Thanks," I said.

"I also brought some horses, in case we wanted to take a ride. All three of us. Delores, you interested?"

"I'd love to go for a ride," she said.

She spun the loaf of bread closed and knotted a bread tie over it.

"Here he comes," Punch said, watching the old man start up the hill.

Woody had to be seventy. He moved with difficulty, but he didn't baby himself. He walked straight up the hill without stopping, his left arm swinging more freely than his right. Maybe a stroke, I thought. His skin, when he got closer, appeared spotted and thin, as if it had worn away in years of weather. His eyes, too, shone red and watery. Any wind at all lifted his hair, which was as thin and fine as milkweed.

I went over and collected Speed and walked him to meet Woody.

"Woody," Punch said, "these are the girls I told you about. That's Delores and this is Hattie."

"From New Hampshire, eh? Well, that's fine."

He didn't shake our hands, but he nodded to us. The bend in his waist kept his eyes low, as if he spent his entire life searching for something he couldn't quite find on the ground in front of him. I walked Speed over to him. Woody lifted his head and inspected him.

"He's a long way from home," Woody said, putting his hand on Speed's forehead. "Aren't you, boy?"

He patted Speed's forehead and then stopped and tried to see Speed's eyes. Speed shook his head. Then Woody walked slowly around Speed, his eyes taking notes. He let his hand trail down Speed's side.

"Walk him in a circle for me, would you, dear?" he asked me.

I did what he asked. Speed obliged me. We walked in a ten-foot circle. When we came back, Woody nodded at me.

"So is he your horse?" Woody asked. "Or do you both own him?"

"We both own him," I said.

"He owns himself," Delores said.

Woody glanced at her. Mostly he looked at the horse.

"And your idea is to pasture him out here for the winter with Fry's herd?" asked Woody.

I nodded.

"Well, it's anyone's guess, of course, how he'll fare," Woody said, his hair lifting in the breeze. "Hard to say. I can tell you he's old, but you know that. I suppose the best thing you can do is let him roam around a little and see what happens. He might surprise you. On the other hand, he might find it too much."

"You don't think he's suffering?" Delores asked.

I looked at her.

"No, I don't think so," Woody answered. "Give him a day or two to get acclimated and see how he responds. Punch here will pull his shoes. He's got the tools in the truck. Give him plenty of water. The winter might be too much for him, but you never know. And Fry's humane about his decisions. He won't let him suffer if it turns bad."

"Thank you," I said.

He stepped past Speed's head and he took my hand. He squeezed. His eyes got wetter, and he nodded.

"We love them so," he said.

I put my free arm around Speed and buried my face in his neck. Woody wiggled my hand just a little, then let it drop and headed back down the hill.

WE FOLLOWED PUNCH WESTWARD, STAYING ON THE RIDGE, the day slowing to afternoon and evening. A cooler wind had picked up and blew from miles of plains. We spotted the wild horses twice. Each time they scattered and swirled, not far, and the males on point scuffed and postured and bluffed. Punch rode easily, his long frame cocked in the saddle. Delores, to her credit, didn't pretend to be a third wheel on a date. She liked riding too much to allow a little romance to interfere with her pleasure. Sometimes she trotted ahead. She sat pretty on a horse. Punch, I imagined, had wondered if we could ride as well as we seemed to think we could, and I felt like we had given a fair accounting of ourselves.

It was a perfect day. The clouds continued to ride and sail, and the sky remained blue and quiet. My horse, a small sorrel named Taffy, possessed a sweet disposition. She preferred the rear, and I didn't goad her forward. We rode in silence most of the way, because a lot of talking seems silly on a horse sometimes. After about an hour we let them drink in the stream that ran through the property. We dismounted and stood listening to water going over stones. The horses drank with their tunnel tongues, and you could see the water hit their bellies.

"We're going to Boston next spring," Punch said. "The rodeo, I mean. That's not too far from New Hampshire, is it?"

"Almost neighbors," Delores said. "Hattie can get to Boston no sweat."

"I'd like to see New Hampshire," Punch said. "You make it sound pretty nice."

Afterward we climbed back up and raced a little. We

didn't go flat out, just sort of cantered, but Taffy buzzed right along, and Spook, Delores's horse, stayed beside her. Arthur, Punch's horse, seemed a little clumsy beside them, but his gait ate ground and he bounced along. We had made it about halfway back when the sun threw our shadows ahead of us. I'm not sure what the others felt, but the moment seemed kind of special, like we were chasing our own ghosts. Our silhouettes danced ahead, and we connected at the horse's hooves, each step mirroring the other in shadow, our bodies elongated and mythic, our shadow horses running ahead of us.

When we crested the last hill, I saw Speed. He stood behind the tent, his head down. He wasn't eating. Mist covered him, and it took me a moment to distinguish him, to be sure he hadn't become a wraith. I let out a shout, and I galloped right at him, and Punch caught my notion and did the same, and so did Delores. We thundered down at him, crazy horses, shadow horses, and for an instant Speed lifted his head and came alive. He snorted and took two steps off as we got closer. *He is indeed a horse,* I thought. I whooped again, and Punch swung his hat around. Delores stood high in her stirrups.

I wanted Speed to run once, just once, to head off free for

the first time in his life. For an instant he looked like he might do it. His posture grew and he shook his head, but as quickly as it had come, it left him. We rode up to him, slamming down to a stop, and he took the wind of our charge and shrank back to being an old horse. Our shadows ran over him, and then the mist caught them and turned them quiet and silver.

Chapter 9

"SOME PEOPLE TRY TO MAKE CHILI AS HOT AS PAINT thinner," Fry said, his good hand stirring a large vat of chili, a beer open in front of him. He stood in a surprisingly clean kitchen in front of a Viking six-burner stove, a blue cook's apron knotted around his neck. He liked to cook, obviously. The wall nearest the window contained more than a hundred cookbooks, most of them with exotic titles you didn't see on a typical cook's shelf. *How to Cook, Clean, and Reuse a Steer. Small Bird Recipes. Crawly Things: The Preparation of Least Meat.* A rack of cooking utensils, all gleaming, hung above the stove. Despite his infirmity, Fry moved around the kitchen gracefully, his good hand reaching accurately for anything he required. He looked at home, and the chili smelled out of this world.

Fry had come up to our campsite to invite us in after we returned from the ride. Punch had taken Woody back to the rodeo with the horses, promising to return in the morning. He also told us that Fry's chili was famous in that part of Minnesota, and that despite Fry's gruff manner, he possessed a generous, open heart. So when we showed up at his door, hungry and looking to be out of the wind that had started blowing at sunset, we weren't sure what to expect. Fry invited us in to sit at a kitchen bar and watch him prepare his famous chili. He said he had started cooking the chili a day and a half before and it was our good fortune that we showed up when we did.

"My uncle Willy makes it hot," Delores said, sitting on a stool and watching him cook, an orange soda open in front of her. "You wouldn't believe it. He calls it five-alarm and makes you sign a release before you eat it."

"Now, no disrespect to your uncle, but that's just the wrong idea," Fry said. "You might as well stick your tongue out and sprinkle chili powder on it. A good chili has to have self-awareness. It has to be content to be what it is, at the same time yearning to be more."

"Come off it," Delores said.

Fry smiled. He seemed to appreciate Delores's blunt manner. It felt as though they had known each other longer than half an afternoon. Delores liked kidding him.

"Do you get cell phone reception here?" I asked. "I probably should call home."

Fry looked up from his stirring.

"Strange thing is, we do. And I have satellite, too. A guy explained to me that cell phone signals jump around. You might have to walk up the hill a little, and sometimes you need to wait until full nightfall, but you can usually get it."

"I'll try it now," I said, "if there's time."

"Well, this will be ready in about fifteen minutes. I have some corn bread in the oven, too. The timing should be about right," Fry said. "Delores, you mind helping me set the table? We'll just eat right here at the bar."

Delores hopped off her stool. I slipped into my barn jacket and stepped outside. The sun had dipped down behind the small rise, and cold air flowed from the west. A few stars had stuttered out of the last sunlight and blinked, slow and steady, as they gained strength. I stayed in the porch light until I dialed. When I heard the phone ringing, I walked up toward our campsite, keeping the phone to my ear. My mom picked up on the third ring.

"Hattie," she said.

"Hello, Mom," I said.

"Now where are you? I've been worried sick."

"We're in Minnesota. We're actually turning around in the next day or so."

"Delores, too?" she asked.

I heard my mom turn a faucet on, then turn it off.

"No, she's going out to Oregon to try things with her dad for a while. That's the plan right now."

"Well, okay. That's probably for the best. And what about the trailer? She's taking that with her?"

"Yes. I'll grab a bus in Blue Earth. That's in Minnesota, right where we are."

"And Speed's going to stay there?"

I couldn't answer. I felt my throat close and my eyes get wet, and my chest felt like someone stood on it.

"What is it, honey?" my mom asked after a second or two. "Is Speed okay?"

"Yes," I said, starting to cry. "I just worry I was selfish to bring him. Maybe I made him suffer more than he needed to and it's my fault if he did. He's not doing great, and I don't think anyone except me thinks he has a prayer of making it through the winter. I just saw it all wrong."

My mom took a deep breath.

"Loving an animal is never wrong, Hattie," she said quietly. "I'm proud of you."

I started crying harder.

"I am," she said softly. "You tried something brave and courageous, and maybe it won't work out quite the way you wanted, but things have a way of curving away from us. You loved that horse. I ran into Mrs. Ferguson at the Stop and Shop the other day . . . and she was so concerned for you and Speed. She said every horsewoman has a *one,* a horse that gets into her heart and stays there to her last day. She said she had a horse named Ali Baba when she was about your age, and she loved that horse more than anything. So she understands, Hattie, and I do, too. Don't take it out on yourself. You did what you thought was best."

I couldn't speak. I felt my heart breaking.

"Is he actually failing?" Mom asked after some more time had passed.

"No," I managed. "Not entirely."

"Where there's life, there's hope, Hattie," she said. "Remember that."

"I will."

"And tell me you're safe."

"I am, Mom. Delores, too. We're going to probably wait

here another day and see if Speed can adjust. We'll walk him down to the herd and see what happens."

"Herd?"

"This man named Fry has a wild horse ranch here. He lets them run free. That was our idea for Speed all along."

"Well, see?" Mom said. "You never know. Miracles happen, Hattie. You're giving Speed a chance, at least."

Neither one of us spoke. Delores came out of the door and called me to dinner. I yelled back that I'd be right there.

"You do me a favor and give Delores a great big hug for me," my mother said. "She's one of my girls, too. You tell her I'll miss her."

"Okay, Mom."

"I'm proud of you. You remember that."

"Thank you, Mom," I said. "I'll call when I find out my connections and the schedule and everything. It will probably take a couple days to get home."

"Okay, sweetheart," she said. "You come home to me safe and sound. I love you."

"Love you," I said, and closed the phone.

▸ ▸ ▸ ▸

IT WAS LATE WHEN THE HORSES CAME.

I felt them first deep down in my spine, the thud of their hooves like the child's game of tapping your friend's back while she tries to speak or sing a silly song. Then for a second the sound disappeared and I woke, or I dreamed, and a minute later, an hour later, the horses reappeared. They came up the hill, their hooves pounding, and I remembered stories I had heard about buffalo shaking the earth when they passed, of miles of black, hairy beasts, and the Sioux and the Crow riding their horses into the stream of buffalo and shooting arrows point-blank into their skulls and necks. Then the animals would fall, another thud, a longer one with a dirty skid, but now, in the night, it was the horses I heard, their hooves like something pounding to be let inside. I felt Delores's hand come onto my shoulder, and she whispered, "Do you hear them?"

The question meant nothing. Sounds and shaking gobbled it up, and Delores slid out of the tent, me right behind, and we stood to find the horses running past. Horses everywhere, horses spooked, horses mad with the autumn night, the chilly stars, the blasting wind that came and turned my feet to ice. Delores grabbed my hand and pulled me next to the trees so I wouldn't be trampled. She let out a wild yell, and I yelled with her, my heart going up and feeling crazy, because we were inside the herd. I smelled horse. Horse created the wind. Horse created the dirt and the stringy flicks of moisture that coated the grass. Horse pounded the hill until it shook and relented.

Delores rocked back and screamed her heart out, and I did, too, and the horses flashed by, white eyes wild and searching, legs prancing and reaching to keep steady on the terrain. "Go, go, go, go," I whispered at the tail end of my shout. And this was why I loved horses. This was why horses were indeed horses and all other jades mere beasts. I bent back and tucked behind the tree, and the horses split around us like water breaking over rock. Delores slipped out her hand from behind the tree, and it took me a second to understand, but then I did. I put my arm out, too, and a second later a horse ran by and shoved my hand hard back at me, then another, my hand sometimes touching cheek, or flank, or tail. I kept my arm slack so that nothing would catch or pull, but instead I was a turnstile feeling the horses pass, not one but twenty, not an individual horse, but all horses. Crazy thoughts spilled through my head, and before I could do anything about them, the horses disappeared. They sucked air after them, left dust, and it took us a second to comprehend what had happened. I turned to Delores and she turned to me, and we hugged without saying a word. We hugged long and hard. And we both knew what it was about. We both knew this was the end of something, and the beginning, and that horses were mixed up in it in ways we'd never be able to explain. I felt her crying, and I cried, too, and then we both saw how nutty it all was and we started to laugh. I felt her body shake and she felt mine, and we pushed away, grinning, and I couldn't help myself. Who would ever be inside a horse herd if not us, and when would we ever be again, and I was still laughing when Delores reached out and yanked me against her again.

"Speed's gone," she whispered into my ear. "He's a horse."

WE CHECKED.

We checked everywhere we could think of, each second's passing providing us with an insane, mad hope.

Speed was gone. He had vanished.

We looked a long time, calling to each other whenever we separated, but we turned up nothing. Afterward we fixed the camp. The horses had trampled things, but the truck and trailer had prevented them from getting too close. A V of horse prints went around our gear and narrowed out below it.

"Fry should have told us they could come up this way,"

Delores said. But she didn't seem angry, and neither was I. But truthfully, we could have been injured.

When we bedded down again, it was nearly morning. Delores had trouble settling. She fluffed half a dozen times the backpack that served as a pillow, her body spinning to find a comfortable spot. Each time she moved, she hit the tent walls and made the sleeping mats whistle.

"Do you think he ran?" I asked, wishing I had seen it, wishing I could know for sure.

"I think he ran," Delores said, finally flopping down. "I think he was a horse for once in his life."

"I can't believe it."

"They just swept him up. He didn't have a choice."

"You really think Speed ran?" I asked again, still having trouble getting my mind around it.

"Did you feel them go by?" she said, not quite answering. "I couldn't believe what they felt like."

"Weird that they were running at night, isn't it?"

"Something could have scared them. You never know. Speedy boy went right with them. I'm telling you."

"I want to see him."

"We can find him tomorrow. Fry said he needed to bring some hay out, and we can ride along. He said they stay down by the stream mostly."

"And Punch will be out."

"And Punch will be out," Delores said, "that's right."

The morning sun turned the top of the tent pale green. It wasn't light as much as the promise of light. I closed my eyes, trying to feel the pounding of the horses again through my back. But they had moved away, and I didn't feel anything except a good wind that blew up and over the hill.

"I'm leaving tomorrow, I think," Delores said. "It's time."

"You mean today?"

"I guess it is today. After we see Speed."

"Okay," I said.

"You're leaving, too, right?" she asked.

"I guess so. I hadn't thought that far ahead."

"Speed made it," she said. "I mean, we won't know for sure until we see him, but it looks like he made it."

"I still can't believe it."

"It was because of you, Hattie," Delores said. "You brought him here. I helped, but you brought him."

"We both brought him."

"Well, I don't know, but here he is. He might surprise us. And I trust Fry to be good with the animals. He'll look after him."

"I trust him, too," I said. "And he makes good chili."

"Amazing chili!" Delores agreed, her voice going up with energy.

"And the corn bread."

She grunted.

"Give me some corn bread," she said, making her voice deep and commanding. "Give me some corn bread *now*."

"I'll remember those horses hitting my hand the rest of my life."

"Me too," Delores said.

"And the way the earth shook."

"Blue earth."

"Yes, blue earth."

A little while later Delores said she loved me.

"I want you to know that," she said. "Whatever happens in the rest of our lives, I want you to know you were my friend."

I rolled closer and hugged her. A cricket landed on the tent wall and stayed there. It buzzed away in the morning light, summer going with it once and for all.

PUNCH AND I RODE IN THE BACK OF FRY'S HALF TON, OUR butts planted on a huge pile of hay bales, our backs against the truck cab. Delores sat in front with Fry, happy to be a supervisor and not a worker. Whenever Fry slowed down,

Punch and I each shot onto our feet and threw a bale over the side. Fry paused a second to let us get our balance and sit back down, then the truck moved on. The hay smelled wonderful, like timothy and sage, but it grated the skin on my forearms. I rolled down the sleeves of my flannel shirt and tucked my fleece closer. After that, I didn't have any problems.

The sun couldn't beat back the cold air that pushed in with each passing hour, and by late morning I felt chilled. Fry's radio claimed we might get a frost that night. The stream appeared now and then in our passage, and fallen leaves clogged any slower-moving water. Twice we spotted the horse herd, but we didn't stop to watch them. I strained to see Speed each time, then the truck moved, and Fry tapped the top of the cap with his good hand, and we continued.

"Don't you worry," Punch said after the second time. "Fry wouldn't be prolonging the tension if he didn't think Speed was okay."

"I just want to see him."

"It's quite a thing," Punch said. "Him coming back to life like that."

"We don't know for sure."

Before Punch answered, Fry stopped the truck.

We jerked to our feet and tossed a bale on either side

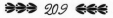

of the truck. I heard Delores singing country-and-western music like a crazy woman. We sat down once we launched the bales. Fry drove on.

"Well, he's around somewhere," Punch said, his body at ease against the truck cab. "He can't get out, and I don't see any buzzards."

"Buzzards?"

"A fact of life, is all, Hattie," he said.

He took my hand as we went along.

By late morning we had nearly emptied the truck, leaving rectangles of hay scattered over most of the acreage. I couldn't be sure, but it dawned on me that Fry had taken a long way around, checking to make sure no animal had gone down. Punch hadn't been kidding about buzzards. Fry hadn't wanted to drive right up to the herd first thing in case the run had been too much for Speed. He had circled around, letting us help him deliver hay, before he swept back and parked the truck above the herd. It was just noon, and the horses grazed in the sun.

Delores jumped out as soon as Fry stopped the truck, and she scrambled up beside us. We had a perfect view of the herd from the back of the truck. The herd stretched down to the stream and into the shade of the trees. I started to count the horses, but gave up after reaching a hundred. Three hundred, I guessed. Maybe less. Five minutes before I would have bet money that I could find Speed in any congregation of horses, seen him no matter what, but I couldn't spot him for the longest time. Each instant I thought I saw him, he disappeared, or the horse under observation blended into the herd and obscured his outline.

"You see him anywhere?" Fry called up.

"Not yet," Delores called back.

"Well, look a little longer, and then we'll head back. He's in there somewhere."

Delores spotted him a few minutes later.

She screamed and pounded the top of the truck.

"Right there, right there." She pointed to the lower left section of the horses. "Right beyond that white one. . . . See him? That's him. There he is."

And it was.

I saw him as he grazed near the back of the herd, his nose pushing grass. He looked different somehow, wilder, but he was still Speed. He ate quietly, his concentration on the food in front of him. He appeared entirely average, just one of the herd, but seeing him made my heart go up. Delores slipped her arm around my waist.

"He's a horse, Hattie," she whispered. "Speed is finally a horse."

"He's beautiful," I said, my eyes filling.

"He's free, and he's part of a herd. That's paradise for a horse," Punch said.

"He ran, I think," I said, and started to cry. "I think he ran with the other horses."

"Sure he did," Delores said.

"And now he's just eating, and all around him he has other horses. And no kids to kick him or tell him to go faster. If he died tomorrow, I wouldn't mind. Not like before," I said.

"I know," Delores said. "It was all worth it."

Then the horses started to move. They didn't sprint or run wildly as they had the night before, but something made them raise their heads and shove off a dozen steps. Speed went, too. He lifted his head and his ears went forward, and for just an instant he ran. His legs lifted and his body soared forward. Delores squeezed my waist. I watched as long as I could, watched until the horses moved on, Speed at the tail of the herd, but part of it, part of everything.

LEANING AGAINST HIS TRUCK, I KISSED PUNCH A LONG KISS at the gate to Fry's land. Punch's truck pointed west. Ours pointed east, into Blue Earth, where Delores would deliver me to the bus station. Punch kissed me and then whispered into my ear that he had enjoyed getting to know me, that he hoped to see me in Boston, that not to worry, Fry knew his horses and he would send word if anything happened to Speed, but that all the signs looked promising, and Fry would do what he could, I could count on it. Then Punch kissed me one more time, said he didn't believe in long goodbyes, couldn't stand them, in fact, and he stepped into his pickup and started it. He waved to Delores, and she waved back. She yelled to say hello to Drew, who was meeting him at the next rodeo stop, but I couldn't be sure he heard her.

"That is one handsome cowboy," she said as I climbed inside the truck.

"He's a great guy."

"We better move it if you're making the bus."

We drove back the way we came, following a country road Punch had recommended. The trailer rattled behind us, less grounded now without Speed to anchor it.

"You got everything you need?" Delores asked me.

"Sure."

"I wish you'd take more of the money. We were supposed to split it fifty-fifty."

"You're going to need some money out in Oregon, Delores. It will all wash out in the end. And if anything goes wrong with the truck on the way there, well, you should have it."

"Okay," she said. "Thank you."

Delores hustled us along, and I watched out the window. I couldn't quite believe it was over. At 3:47 I would climb on a bus and head back east, and in a day or two, not much longer, I would end up in White River Junction, Vermont, not far from where we started. My mom would pick me up, and she would be nice, interested, but she would let her concern about my future creep in, and pretty soon we'd start gnawing on each other again. Mostly, though, I felt like life had taken a turn, one I couldn't quite understand yet, but that something was happening whether I wanted it to or not. And I thought of Speed, too, who had probably figured his life was over, if he thought at all, but in a week's time he ended up on a ranch in Minnesota, a wild horse. You couldn't know what might happen.

"I miss him," I said.

"Who?" Delores asked, grabbing a plug of bubble gum and unwrapping it with her teeth. "Speed or Punch?"

"Speed."

"I know," she said. "It's weird without him around."

"You going to call your dad soon and say you're on your way?"

She nodded. Her jaw flexed with her chewing. She crumpled up the wrapper and dropped it onto the seat.

"It will work," I said.

"I hope so. If it doesn't, I don't know what I'll do."

"You'll just come back and live with me."

"Oh, your mom would love that."

"She loves you and you know it," I said.

"Paulette's going to love having you back."

"She'll hate me because I haven't called."

"She'll get over it."

Delores rolled down her window and spit out the bubble gum.

"I swear bubble gum is only good for about a minute," she said. "But I love it anyway."

"Can I ask you something serious?" I said.

"Shoot."

"A while back Mrs. Ferguson talked to me about being a veterinary assistant. Not for dogs or cats but for large animals. You know. Horses and cattle. There's a program at the University of New Hampshire. She thinks I could probably get in on a provisional basis. My grades suck, but I have the GED and she says they need people. What do you think?"

Delores looked at me.

"You could not do anything better in this world, Hattie Wyatt," she said, her eyes on me. "You'd be perfectly suited. I mean it. And you might decide to be a vet yourself."

"One thing at a time," I said.

"No one loves animals like you, Hattie. You do that. You ask Mrs. Ferguson to help you get into the program. She can pull some strings. People like her have lots of strings."

"I think it'll be good, too."

She reached over and grabbed my hand.

Fifteen minutes later we pulled up to the bus station. It wasn't much—just a ticket window with a tiny waiting room. A bus idled, its exhaust blue-green in the late-afternoon light. Greyhound. Delores unloaded my stuff while I went to the window and bought a one-way ticket. A chubby guy told me to get a move on, the bus was about to leave. I grabbed the ticket and ran back outside.

"It's my bus," I said.

Delores carried my backpack. I carried my carry-on bag. The bus driver, a tall, thin broom of a man, threw the other passengers' bags into the undercarriage. He slammed the doors down.

Delores took me in her arms. I squeezed her as hard as I could.

"You're a woman going west," I said. "No one can stop you."

She nodded against me.

"Load it up," the bus driver shouted.

I grabbed my backpack from Delores and lugged it step by step up the stairs. I dropped the bags onto the first empty seat I found and knelt to look out the window. The bus made a releasing sound, the brakes sighing, and I strained left and right to see Delores. I saw her as the bus pulled away. She had her hand up, waving, but I wasn't sure she could see me through the tinted windows.

Chapter 10

IT COULD HAVE EASILY BEEN LOST.

The postcard arrived in a bunch of other mail, and some-how it had tucked down into the *Pennysaver*, a local shopper newspaper that called itself the North Country's best flea market. The mail sat on the seat of my old Chevy pickup, a two-wheel-drive S-10, because I had grabbed the letters on my way out of the house. Most of the mail was addressed to my mother.

I probably wouldn't have noticed the card except that I had gotten cold tending to the horses and had decided to eat my lunch in the truck with the heater going. It was April and rainy, the last of the snow peeling away under the large drops of moisture. The Fergusons had left me in charge of the horses while they played golf in Bermuda. Mud season held the barn in a soggy, wet cast. Whenever the horses moved, their hooves pulled up large sucks of mud that splattered their bellies. They looked like brown-spotted dalmatians.

I was more interested in the mail these days because I had been accepted into the veterinary assistant program, large animals, at the University of New Hampshire. The acceptance had come bundled with provisions. I had to maintain a 2.7 GPA. I had to complete a summer internship. If my grades slipped below thus and so, I would be bounced. I was part of a North Country statewide outreach program. Whatever it was called, once the University of New Hampshire had gotten the idea I was attending the following fall, mail came by the bucketfuls.

I didn't check the mail for letters from Delores. She called or texted late at night to tell me about her dad, her job at Home Depot, the boy she had started dating.

When I lifted the *Pennysaver* to take a look at it, the postcard from Fry slipped out. My heart stopped. The peanut butter and jelly sandwich I had been eating turned to stones in my mouth. I swallowed as best I could.

I looked at the card. I saw my address and the address of the sender. The front side of the card had a chili recipe on it. I turned off the truck and stepped out into the wet mist. I tucked the card into my back pocket.

I made myself finish mucking out the stables. I raked out old hay and replenished three stalls with new bedding. The horses nodded and dozed. I worked for most of the afternoon. The card remained in my back pocket. A hundred times I reached my hand down to check it. Each time my hand fell away from it.

It was nearly sunset when I finished with the stables. I put away the rakes and brushes the way Mrs. Ferguson liked them to be stored. Then I sat on a small bench outside Fabio's stall. He was a big horse, a palomino whose white forelock dangled almost to his eyes. He was a friendly, slightly silly horse. I pulled the card out of my back pocket and tucked it against my knee facedown. I took a deep breath and turned it over.

> *Dear Hattie,*
>
> *Sorry to tell you, your horse stopped running today. We found him when we went out to deliver hay. I can't tell you much about how it happened. He was down when we found him, that's all. He seemed like a*

good horse, and you should be happy he made it to spring. I would have had Punch write to you, but he's down in Arizona, as you likely know. Most of the mares have foaled, and it's some pretty to watch.

Hope you're well.

Regards,

Fry

I stood and put my arms around Fabio's neck. He made a good horse sound, a deep rumbling in his throat and chest, and I hugged him as hard as I could. He nodded his head a little. I whispered that I loved Speed, always would, that he was my boy, that of all the horses that ever were, ever would be, Speed was my *one true horse.* He was the one I thought of when I thought of all horses, and I could recall his face faster than I could any other creature I had ever met. "My one true horse," I whispered. I hoped he had seen the grass turn as green as flame and had breathed the wind carrying the mares' scents, and maybe he'd seen the foals, all candle-legged, their rock-a-horse trotting bringing warmth to his old heart. I buried my face in Fabio's neck and I cried as I had never cried. I cried for everything sad in the world, and for Speed, and for all the things and people who got old and tired, for the good hearts that tried to go on but couldn't. I cried for Delores and I cried for me, and Fabio took it all. He took it all and it went deep into his body, but he didn't move or judge. He accepted my tears and he leaned into me, his great, quiet skin smelling of barns beyond counting, smelling of hay and summer and the knobby oats he loved so much.

And for just a second Fabio became Speed.

"Spring," I whispered, when even old bones get up and walk. And I told him what my first riding instructor told me— that when a horse dies, he becomes Pegasus, the greatest of all horses, a horse with wings, a horse that eats air and canters on light. He soars above the land, free from this world, and I would meet him someday, I promised. We would ride in the sky, and we would perform great deeds, and anyone seeing us would marvel at the magnificence of the horse with wings.

I told him goodbye for Delores and for the Fergusons and even for the children who didn't understand what they had asked of him, what their impatient heels had done to his heart. I explained that I would tell Delores and we would remember him.

"My one true horse," I whispered.

His soul flew up. I saw it in the mist and cold rain. In the late-afternoon light I saw great wings push free of his shoulder blades, and watched evening light shatter and pull to colors along his body. And what had been Speed, this slow, cobby horse, rose and became something shimmering and blinding. No sooner had he left the ground than a sound filled every corner of the world, and a thousand horses, a million horses, all the horses that ever were, stampeded through the sky. And I saw Speed fly up, triumphant at last, and he did not veer left, and he did not stop, and the sparks of his hooves became the dew of evening's first hour.

JOSEPH MONNINGER has published eleven novels and three nonfiction books for adults, as well as three acclaimed novels for young adults: *Wish; Hippie Chick,* a *Bulletin* Blue Ribbon Book; and *Baby,* an ALA-YALSA Top Ten Best Book for Young Adults. He lives in New Hampshire, where he is an English professor.

DATE DUE
